VILLAINS AND VIXENS

THE J.R. FINN SAILING MYSTERY SERIES

C.L.R. DOUGHERTY

VILLAINS AND VIXENS

The J.R. Finn Sailing Mystery Series
Book 5

Vigilante Justice in Florida and the Bahamas

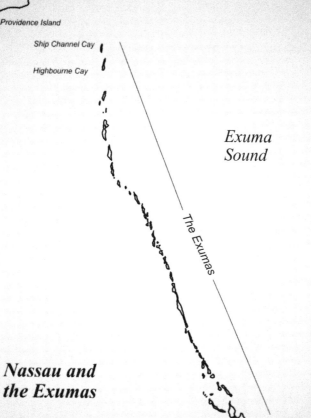

Nassau

New Providence Island

Ship Channel Cay

Highbourne Cay

Exuma
Sound

The Exumas

Nassau and
the Exumas

George Town

Great Exuma Island

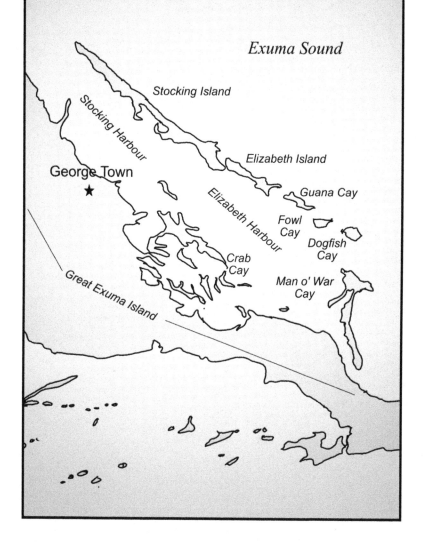

George Town, Great Exuma Island

Exuma Sound

Stocking Island

Stocking Harbour

George Town

★

Elizabeth Island

Guana Cay

Elizabeth Harbour

Fowl Cay

Dogfish Cay

Crab Cay

Man o' War Cay

Great Exuma Island

1

MY TARGET WAS IN THE TOWNHOUSE. I SAW LIGHTS TURNING ON and off in different windows during my two-plus hours of surveillance, and there was movement behind the Venetian blinds.

There was only one entrance — two if you counted the attached garage. No one arrived or departed while I was watching. It was nine p.m. now — a little late for a casual, unannounced visit, but not late enough to cause alarm. I decided to go for it.

I locked my rental car and walked the hundred yards to the front door of the townhouse. It took us over a month to track her to this place in Gainesville, Florida, in a neighborhood near the University. It was a nice place, given that it was in an area catering to the college crowd. The market for these town-houses must be faculty members. They were a bit too upscale for students, by my reckoning.

I was dawdling as I approached the front door, anxious as I thought about what might happen in the next minute or two.

This could be one of those "kill or be killed" moments. Stepping onto the little porch, I took a deep breath and knocked.

"Coming," a woman's voice called, her tone cheerful, even expectant. I heard a security chain sliding free, and then the clunk of a deadbolt being drawn. The door opened, and the woman's jaw dropped when she saw me. A whole gamut of emotions played across her face in a split second.

"Finn." She frowned; her jaws clenched.

"Were you expecting someone?" I asked.

"Not you," she said, shaking her head.

"No, I guess not."

"How did you find me?" she asked.

"Aren't you going to invite me in?"

Her gray eyes were icy as she took her time, looking me up and down. After several seconds, she stepped back and swung the door open. I went inside, and she locked the door, replacing the security chain. She squeezed past me in the small foyer and went into the living room.

"Have a seat," she said, motioning to a brown leather couch in the middle of the open-plan living room. "I need to take care of something. I'll be right back." She went up a staircase as I settled into the cushions.

While she was gone, I didn't drop my guard. She might come back shooting. In my 20-odd years as an assassin, she was the most dangerous woman I ever encountered.

Retired from a small, obscure group in the Department of Defense, a group that handled government-sanctioned assassinations, I now work for an organization called Phorcys. Founded by several retired senior U.S. military officers, Phorcys is committed to cleaning up rampant corruption that reaches to the highest levels in our government.

My mission tonight was unusual. I didn't normally

socialize with my targets before I executed them, but this woman was different. She was an enigma; we weren't sure what to make of her.

"You should have called first," she said, coming back into the room after a couple of minutes. "I had plans for the evening." She scowled at me, then stared over my shoulder.

"I didn't know if you would take my call," I said, as I glanced behind me, making a quick visual sweep of the room. I wondered what she was looking at, but nothing caught my eye.

The furnishings were tasteful, expensive looking. But there were no personal touches. Did she pay a decorator to furnish this place? "And I didn't have your number, anyway."

"You shouldn't have dropped in like this."

"How long do we have?" I asked.

She frowned. "Before what?"

"Before your guest comes." I was fishing; when she came to the door, she acted as if she were expecting company. "Or did you reschedule?"

"That's not any of your business, Finn."

"Maybe not," I said, "but since you mentioned plans, I thought I'd ask."

"I don't owe you an explanation," she said.

"No?"

"No. What makes you think you're entitled to show up unannounced like this, after all this time?"

"The way we parted in Charleston."

I last saw Mary a little over a month ago, in Charleston, South Carolina. We were working together then. Or at least, that's what I thought, along with the others who made up Phorcys. She and I were their front-line troops. When all else failed, they deployed the two of us to eliminate dishonest bureaucrats and politicians, as well as the occasional plain old crook. We were also a couple, which introduced its own set of complications.

She was abducted as she was staking out one of our intended targets. I intercepted her captors as they were delivering her to a yacht belonging to a Russian gangster. I rescued her. She was a little dopey from the drugs her kidnappers gave her, but otherwise, she seemed all right. I took her to our hotel to let her recover, but that night she slipped out of our room.

I found her again the next morning. During the time she was on her own, she went after the Russian. She talked her way aboard his motor yacht, only to find that he wasn't there. Frustrated in her quest for personal vengeance, she killed the entire crew of his yacht — the very people he expected to capture her.

That derailed our mission. Consulting with Phorcys, we decided to regroup and let things settle down. We left town separately, planning to meet in St. Thomas a week later. When Mary didn't show up, our employer and I began looking for her. Given what happened in Charleston, we assumed the Russian was behind her disappearance.

Two days ago, we found her here in Gainesville, living in this townhouse. I was here to find out what she was doing, and to deal with her as I thought appropriate.

"Don't be cryptic, Finn. What are you talking about? The way we parted? I'm confused."

"You aren't the only one. When you dropped me off at the airport in Charleston, we were expecting to meet in St. Thomas in a week. Like you said, that was over a month ago."

She frowned. "St. Thomas?"

"In the U.S. Virgin Islands."

"I know where it is. Why were we meeting there?"

"You wanted to sail to Isla de Aves and chill out for a while. We were between missions, after what happened in Charleston."

"You and I were there once, weren't we? At Isla de Aves?" She had a faraway look on her face. "On a boat?"

"We were, yes." *This is surreal. Is she playing some mind game with me?*

"That was your boat, wasn't it? What was she called? *Island Girl*? Or something about a princess?"

"Both. Her name is *Island Girl,* but we changed it to *Carib Princess* for a little while."

"Why did we do that?"

"We were on the run," I said.

"Um ... From Rory O'Hanlon, right?" she asked, nodding. "And Frankie Dailey. I met you in Puerto Rico, didn't I?"

I struggled to make sense of what she was saying. Taken individually, the pieces of information she tossed out were correct, but the context was garbled. She had things out of order, and there were lengthy periods of time between the occurrences she referred to.

"What's going on with you, Mary?"

"Kathy," she said.

"What?"

"Kathy. Short for Kathleen. I'm not Mary now."

"Okay," I said. "Kathleen Riley, right?"

"Yes. How did you know that?"

I'll just let you wonder about that for now. Two can play this game. "When did you start using that identity?"

"I don't know, exactly. I used it all through college, so when I came back here, I picked it up again. I came here because I needed time with Sam."

"Who is Sam?"

"I'm not telling you that. Maybe soon, but not just yet."

"I see."

"No, you don't."

"Okay. Whatever you say."

"I'm in control," she said.

"Yes, you are." *This gets stranger and stranger.* "All right. Tell me why you didn't come to St. Thomas."

"Okay. Sam says I'm ready, but I don't feel ready."

"Ready? Ready for what?"

"To deal with everything. Don't push me, okay?"

"Sorry. I don't understand, but I'm trying."

"I know. I've had some problems, but Sam's helped me figure things out. Now I just have to piece everything together. Sam said it would help if I could talk with you about it all. But I wanted more time. I'll try to tell you what's happened."

"Okay." I nodded.

"Before I start, can I get you a drink? Coffee? Wine? Anything?"

"I'm okay for now, thanks."

I held Mary's gaze as she took several deep breaths. After a few seconds, she raised her eyebrows. I nodded, and she began her story.

2

"ALL RIGHT, THEN. HERE GOES. I'LL START WITH CHARLESTON. IN layman's terms, I flipped out after I left you at the airport."

In layman's terms?

She looked me in the eye, waiting for my reaction, her lips pursed. I kept my expression neutral and nodded for her to go ahead.

"Sam says I was suffering from what's called a Brief Psychotic Disorder. It was probably triggered by being drugged and kidnapped. It was aggravated by my killing those people that same day. Twelve people, on that big boat, you remember? I blew them away without even a minute's thought. Twelve people. And I left a bloody, gruesome mess. But I think they deserved it."

"*Anastasia*," I said.

"That was the motor yacht?"

"Yes, that's right."

"It belonged to a Russian gangster, didn't it?" she asked.

"Yes, it did. And you're right; those people deserved to die."

"Okay. Those things help. I have a lot of disjointed memories that I'm trying to put together. I've got a decent grasp of what happened after Charleston, but before is a jumble."

"Okay," I said.

"About the killings. To me, it doesn't matter that they deserved it."

"No?" *Is she remorseful? That's not the woman I know.*

"No. I acted on pure impulse. I didn't think things through; I just went wild. I lost it. I wasn't professional."

"Uh-huh," I said, nodding. *Not remorse for the killings. Regret for acting on the spur of the moment.* "Maybe so, but you still did a professional job. No evidence left behind; nobody has a clue what happened. The cops think it was the Russian and his enforcer who did it. But those two have disappeared."

"You got that from those people?"

"Those people? I'm lost. Which people?"

"The ones we were working for."

So you remember something about that.

We were both new to Phorcys, although Mary started working with them before I did. She was involved in recruiting me, but neither of us realized that at the time. Mary, despite her youth, was a well-established contract killer. We made a good team, she and I did. Or so we all thought.

In one of those bizarre quirks of fate, her uncle was one of the founders of Phorcys. Lt. General Bob Lawson, U.S.A. Retired, — her Uncle Bob. Bob was also the man who recruited me from the Army twenty-odd years earlier to join that secret group within the DoD.

Bob's sister, Mary's mother, was a drug-addicted prostitute. Despite Bob's efforts to help her, she succumbed to an overdose, leaving Mary to fend for herself at age twelve. Mary had a rough life, growing up on her own. Bob tried to help, but she wasn't receptive.

By the time Bob joined with some of his colleagues to form Phorcys, Mary was making a living as a killer for hire. That was how she paid her way through college.

Because of Bob, Phorcys began using her for the occasional job. Within a few months, they were keeping her busy full time, although she was still a contractor when they sent her to watch over me. But that's another story. Several other stories, in fact.

"Yes. I got that from Phorcys," I said, in answer to her question. "Aaron, specifically."

"Right. Aaron," she said. "Your old Army buddy. Hernandez?"

"No, Sanchez. Aaron Sanchez."

Aaron Sanchez was the intelligence officer within Phorcys, and an old friend of mine from our early days in the army. Before Aaron became part of Phorcys, he was the intelligence officer for that group I worked in at the DoD.

"And did he and his people find me? Did Phorcys send you to bring me back?"

"There's more to it than that, M-Kathy. But yes, he found you. Don't let me get you off the track. My story can wait."

"Okay, but I want you to tell me everything, once I finish." She nodded once and took a deep breath, then said, "Brief Psychotic Disorder is a rare thing, I'm told. Have you heard of the Diagnostic and Statistical Manual of Mental Disorders? DSM-5, it's called."

"Heard of it, but that's all," I said. "Why?"

"Brief Psychotic Disorder is described in there. There are several symptoms: delusions, paranoia, hallucinations, that kind of thing. That's what most people think of when they hear 'psychosis.' But mood changes and disorganized thinking

are part of the package, too. That's me. Disorganized thinking — it sounds simple, but ... "

She shook her head. "When you're caught up in this web of
conflicting — oh, hell, Finn. I can't describe it. Up seems like
down, but then all of a sudden you think it's not down, but it's
sideways, or inside out. That doesn't make any sense, but ... "

"I'll take your word for it," I said, shaking my head.

She cleared her throat. "I freaked out after you got on that
plane in Charleston. I was scared out of my mind."

"You? Scared? Why?"

"You were the only person I trusted; the only one I ever
remember trusting. And you left me."

"You wanted me to leave you. You were the one who
decided to stay in Charleston while I went ahead to Tortola.
You wanted to take care of some things while I got the boat
ready, you said."

She nodded, frowning. "I believe you, but I can't
remember that. It seems odd that I would want you to leave
when I was afraid without you. But that's why it's called
crazy, I guess. I'm not supposed to use that word, crazy.
But ... shit! I was crazy then. That's all there is to it; I was
crazy."

She paused, looking down at her hands. She picked at the
cuticle on her left thumb and shook her head. After several
seconds, she looked up at me.

"After you left, I came back here. The University's the only
place that ever felt like home, see? My college years were the
most stable period of my life. I wanted that sense of security
back. I needed a place to hole up and lick my wounds, get my
bearings again. And Sam's here.

"Now that I've been seeing Sam, I've been working on
putting all the broken pieces back together.

"I want to recover what we had, Finn. Can you forgive me for running out on you?"

"Yes, but there's more to it than my forgiving you. Resuming our life together involves more than just you and me. Have you worked that out, yet?"

"You mean Phorcys?" she asked.

"Phorcys is part of it, for sure. And there's Lavrov, and the rest of the bad guys, the ones from O'Hanlon's list. You remember all that?"

"Yes and no. I remember pieces of it, and the more you say, the more I recall. I can't say I've worked it out yet, but I'm not ignoring them — Phorcys or the others. I've been trying to rank my problems, put the things that are most important to me first. You understand? I lost all that when I broke down. You're the most important part of my life, Finn. If I can recover with you, I can deal with the rest. If I haven't lost you."

"You haven't lost me, but don't underestimate how tough those other things will be."

"I'm working on that. But it would help if you could refresh my understanding. Have I told you enough for now? Enough so you're willing to tell me how you found me? And why you came looking? I would like to think it's because you love me, but I know there's more to it than that. And I need to deal with the reality of my situation. What have I missed since Charleston?"

"All right. That's fair, but can I change my mind about that offer of wine?"

She nodded. "Red or white?"

"Red, if it's handy."

She got up and went into the kitchen. While I was alone, I thought about where to begin, and how much I should tell her. I was on new ground with "Kathy."

I played back my discussions with the others at Phorcys when we were wondering what we should do about Mary. Of all the things we considered to explain her behavior, a psychotic break wasn't one. I came here prepared for almost anything but what I found. When I knocked on her front door, I was ready to kill her, or be killed by her. But life with this woman was never that simple; I should have known that.

The woman I knew as Mary was tough, but "Kathy" was an unknown quantity. She seemed a bit frail and uncertain compared to Mary. I didn't want to precipitate another breakdown; it could have consequences beyond our personal relationship.

3

I COULD HEAR MARY — *I NEED TO CALL HER KATHY TO HER FACE, damn it.* — opening cabinets and drawers. There was the rattle of glassware followed by a musical ringtone from a cellphone. I heard her answer the phone, and then there was the sound of a door closing. *That's probably Sam, whoever the hell he is. Somebody from her college days, I guess.*

Nobody within Phorcys, including her Uncle Bob, knew what she was up to. The woman was a walking time bomb. If she spilled what she knew, the consequences would be dire, not just for those of us in Phorcys, but for the good old U.S. of A.

My current assignment was to evaluate the risk she posed and deal with her accordingly. The executive committee within Phorcys included Bob Lawson and another, slightly older, retired general named Mike Killington. Mike was a legend in the special ops world when I was coming along, and he was Bob Lawson's mentor. I spent the better part of last week with the two of them and Aaron Sanchez as we tried to figure out what to do about Mary.

This wasn't the first time she took off on her own — went off the reservation, as Aaron put it — but it was by far the most serious. As much as Bob Lawson and I wanted to protect her for personal reasons, we acknowledged that she could be dangerous to us.

The only innocent explanation for her absence that we could imagine was that Lavrov, the Russian gangster who kidnapped her, was holding her prisoner, or worse. And then Aaron tracked her down in Gainesville, Florida. We knew the University was her alma mater, but nobody realized she still had ties here.

The situation in which we found her was damning. She was living alone, not a prisoner at all. That foreclosed the only acceptable explanation for her recent disappearance. Had she changed sides? Or taken a contract with somebody else? We didn't know. Either of those things meant I would have to kill her. Or try to, at least. She was a formidable target. I knew her skills better than anybody.

And now, typical of her, she threw our plans into disarray. Nobody considered that she might have lost her marbles. That made her even more dangerous, in a way. On the other hand, if it were true, and if she could recover, well ... We would have to see how things played out.

When I knocked on her door a little while ago, I was hoping to discover that she was being held against her will somehow — that she was a prisoner in this townhouse. Otherwise, my mission was to dispose of her. I was primed for a black or white situation, but now I was dazzled by all the colors of the rainbow. I didn't know what to do, and there was no way to consult with Phorcys before I made a decision.

I knew two things for sure. One, I was no psychiatrist. I couldn't evaluate this whole "brief psychotic disorder" claim.

And two, I dared not leave her unsupervised. We all knew how readily she could disappear; it was one of the things that made her so good at what she did.

"Hey, Finn?" She held a tray with an open bottle of wine, two full glasses, and a plate of fruit and cheese with crackers.

"Yes?"

"Sorry for the interruption. That was Sam. I rescheduled our date for tomorrow. Ready to tell me what you've been up to since Charleston?"

"There's not a lot to tell," I said, taking the wineglass that she passed me. I pretended to take a sip; no way would I risk drinking it, since I didn't see her pour it. "I went to Tortola and got *Island Girl* ready to launch. Then I went on to Charlotte Amalie and dropped the hook in that anchorage on the northwest corner of Water Island. When the time came to meet your flight, I took the dinghy across to the marina in Crown Bay and got a taxi to the airport."

"So you had flight details for me, then?" she looked puzzled.

"You sent them to me in a text — from your encrypted phone to mine."

"Those phones Phorcys gave us, you mean?" she asked.

"That's right."

"I don't remember that. How long between the time I sent the text and the time I was supposed to get there?"

"Thirty hours," I said.

"Thirty hours? You know to the hour?"

"Yes. When you didn't show up, I tried to get in touch with you using the Phorcys phone, but you didn't answer. The phone didn't go to voicemail, either. I checked our blind email drop, but there was nothing from you there. That's when I got worried and called Aaron. He tried to locate your phone, but tracking was disabled. Do you still have the phone?"

She shook her head, frowning. "No. And I remember nothing about any of that. Not making the travel arrangements, nor sending you the text — nothing."

"What did you do with the phone?"

She pursed her lips, tapping them with her finger. After several seconds, she shook her head. "I have no idea. Until you mentioned it, I didn't even recall having that phone. But I remember it, now. I wonder ... " she shook her head again. "I don't know, Finn. So Phorcys started looking for me then? Like, within a few hours of my scheduled arrival time?"

"That's right. And there was no trace of you. Not under any identities that we knew about."

"And when did you find me?"

"In the afternoon, the day before yesterday. Aaron and Bob came up with the idea of following your trail from the University, from the time you graduated. Aaron was hoping to pick up some new false identities to trace. The first problem was that we didn't know what name you were using back then, when you were in college. That prompted Bob to dig out the old private surveillance reports he commissioned when you went missing as a kid."

"You mean after I skipped out of the foster care system? That far back?"

"Yes, exactly. Once Aaron learned that you used the Kathleen Riley identity the whole time you were in college, everything fell into place. You even lived here, in this townhouse, back then. Classy for a college kid, wasn't it?"

"Well, yes. But I wasn't a typical college kid, either. You know that."

"We were surprised you still had access to this place. And

that it wasn't rented, or anything." I looked around. "But it's sort of, I don't know, sterile? Is that the right word? It doesn't look lived in."

"No. Sterile is a good word to describe it. I kept it because I really was planning to come back to graduate school, at some point. And the Kathleen Riley identity is clean, too."

"Don't be too sure of that," I said.

"Why? Has Aaron blown that cover? Or you?"

"No. But he did discover Lavrov's looking for you. That shouldn't be a surprise, after what you did to his people on *Anastasia*."

"Lavrov," she said, staring into the distance. "The Russian. He'll never find me here. Has Phorcys turned up any more intel on him?"

"Some. Mostly just that he's still around. Nothing definitive, except word's out that he's looking for you. You should assume he can find you. If we found you, he can, too."

"But you had the background reports from Bob, back when he was trying to find me after my mother died."

"Yes. That made it a little easier for us, but you were here at the University for over four years. That's a long time; you would have left quite a trail."

"As Kathy Riley, yes. But she was just a student."

"A student who had plenty of cash, from the looks of this place. She was renting it from a shell corporation, too — a little strange for a college kid. And then, given how you were earning money, there was extended travel and unexplained absences. Aaron picked up all that; he was suspicious of Kathleen Riley, but he couldn't be sure until he got the info from the detective who worked for Bob."

"Lavrov won't have access to that," she said.

"No, but he might not be as worried about making a

mistake as we were. He would grab you just on the chance you might be the one he's looking for."

"It's not going to work, Finn."

"What?"

"You're trying to spook me, get me to run back to Phorcys."

"Don't take this the wrong way," I said, "but that may not be an option for you."

"It's not?" Her brows shot up, her eyes round.

"It's not a sure thing." I shook my head.

"Then why are you here, if not to bring me back?"

"Bob and I feel a personal obligation to you."

"I hear a but ... " she said, her eyes narrowing to slits. I held her gaze and kept quiet. She stared at me for several seconds and then spoke.

"Did they send you, Finn? Or is this something you and Bob are doing on your own?"

"It doesn't work that way. Bob and I are attached to you, for personal reasons. But put that aside for a moment and look at this objectively. You know a lot of potentially damaging information, and your disappearance didn't inspire confidence."

She nodded her head and swallowed, hard. Picking up her wineglass, she took a sip and stared into space. "Okay. I get it. I screwed up. Is that it?"

"That's one way to interpret your actions."

"Was it killing the people on *Anastasia*? On my own account?"

"By itself, that may have been a mistake, but it's one that we could live with. Given the situation you were in, you might have made a professional judgment to go on the offensive to protect yourself. That was a decision that was yours to make. None of us would question it."

"But I didn't make a conscious decision, Finn. I lost it; I was

pissed off because I let myself get snatched off the street. I
killed twelve people, basically in a temper tantrum."

"So you say. But they were part of the team that
kidnapped you; they were working for Lavrov. You didn't kill
twelve innocent bystanders. And you're the only one who can
decide whether that was the right thing to do. Phorcys will
live with your call on that one; they've already told you so,
remember?"

"No, I don't remember. They told me that? When?"

"Bob covered that with you when you called in right after
you and I had breakfast at the marina that morning after you
killed them all. You don't remember that?"

She shook her head. "No. Were you on that call?"

"No, but Mike and Bob both told me about it. The
slaughter on *Anastasia* wasn't something they would have
ordered, but they hired you because you brought a different
perspective to situations like that. We all respect your judgment on that. You're the only one who's second-guessing yourself. And I understand that. It's a healthy reaction in my
opinion. But now that you've worked your way through it, put
it to rest. It's done; it can't be undone. Learn what you can from
it and move on."

"You said that wasn't a problem by itself," she said. "The
killings. I'm not sure where you were going with that. Did you
mean it was a problem in some overall context?"

"I meant that it could be, yes. It was the immediate
precursor to your disappearance. That worried us."

"Because I disappeared? Is that it?"

"You killed twelve people you weren't ordered to kill while
you were supposed to be working for Phorcys, and then you
cut and ran. Either of those acts would have raised eyebrows,
but together, they set off alarms. Think about it. We wondered

what the hell you were up to. Were you working for somebody else? Or did Lavrov snatch you again?

"We didn't think you just took off on your own. But then we discovered Lavrov was looking for you, so we knew he wasn't responsible for your disappearance.

"And once we picked up your trail, we started trying to come up with an explanation. None of the plausible reasons for your behavior were favorable for your continued relationship with Phorcys."

She took a big swallow of wine and stared off into space again. After almost thirty seconds, she spoke. "Finn?"

"Yes?"

"I love you, and I know you love me. I need a straight answer to a simple question. Okay?"

"Okay. Ask it."

"Are you here to kill me?"

4

I FORCED MYSELF TO BREATHE AT A NORMAL RATE, RELAXING THE muscles in my jaw. Dropping my gaze to the top of her chest, I fixed my eyes on the triangle of flesh exposed at her collar. If she were going to try a preemptive strike, the first sign would be a twitch in her upper pectoral muscles.

Brute strength and experience were in my favor, but she was faster than I was. I wouldn't kill her — not now, not based on what I knew so far — but she didn't know that. If she attacked, I wasn't at all sure of the outcome.

We sat there watching each other for what seemed like an eternity. My thoughts were racing as I considered how to answer her. She knew the score; there was no chance I could bullshit her.

If I told her they sent me to kill her, only one of us would leave the townhouse alive. I wasn't making any bets on who it would be. If I told her I wasn't sent to kill her, she would think I was lying, and the outcome would be the same.

"I'm going to take a drink of wine before I answer you," I said, playing for time.

She didn't respond.

"I'll move slowly; I don't want to alarm you, okay?"

"Okay," she said, tension in her voice.

I lifted the wineglass to my lips and faked taking a sip. Lowering the glass slowly, I brought it to rest in my lap, cradled in both hands.

"Answer me, please," she said, her voice cracking. "Yes or no?"

"I wasn't given an order to kill you. My mission was to evaluate your situation and make my own decision. To be honest, I was hoping to find you were being held here against your will."

"Why were you hoping that?"

"It was the only explanation we could think of that would excuse your behavior. Anything else would have left us doubting your trustworthiness. Then I would have been expected to kill you, but it was to have been my decision."

She stared at me; her eyes narrowed to slits as she thought about what I said.

"'It was to have been?' You phrased that carefully," she said.

"I tried to; I can't lie to you. Not about something like that."

She took a deep breath and let it out slowly, her eyes relaxing. "Okay. You didn't lie, but you didn't answer me."

"No, not yes-or-no, I didn't. But I told you the truth. None of us wants you dead."

"I believe that, but you haven't decided yet, have you?"

"No, I haven't."

"Why not?"

"You've given me new information; it changes the whole situation."

"I see. Well, I don't think there's much more I can tell you, so I guess you need to fish or cut bait."

"There may not be much more you can tell me, but before I

decide, I need to learn more about this 'brief psychotic disorder' you have."

"And how do you plan to do that? What is it you expect to
learn?"

"It's outside my experience; this is the first time I've even
heard of such a thing. So I need to know what it means to
Phorcys. Does it make you more dangerous to us? Can it
explain what you've done? Is it something you can get over,
and if so, is it likely to happen again? See what I mean?"

She nodded and took a sip of her wine. "What will you do
when you have those answers? Or how will you know whether
to trust the answers? We both know shrinks don't guarantee
the accuracy of their diagnoses. And who are you even going
to ask, anyway?"

"You've done a good job of describing my problem, except
for one other thing."

"What one other thing?"

"I can't leave you alone while I go chasing after answers;
you're too good at disappearing."

She smiled, a sad smile, and nodded. "Yeah. I can't blame
you for feeling that way. You have a responsibility to the
others. I get that."

I wanted to keep her talking; the longer we conversed, the
less likely she would be to attack. At least that was my hope.
"How did you discover you had this 'brief psychotic disorder'
thing? Can you tell me about that?"

"I'm no psychiatrist. I can tell you what I know about it,
though. But first, I want to know where your head is on this
whole thing. You laid out your problem in a bunch of questions. We both know some of them will have ambiguous
answers. But depending on which way the answers tip the

scales, you'll either kill me or bring me back into the fold. Is that right?"

"Yes. But you know that I hope it's the latter, that you're still part of the team. You know that, don't you?"

"It's a relief to hear you say it; it's what I was hoping was hidden in those questions. I can't guess which way the others will vote, but at least I know you're not trying to railroad me."

"You should know that. All of us like you; nobody's happy with this situation, and I know you aren't either."

She nodded, but she said nothing for several seconds. She swirled the wine around in her glass, studying it. Then she looked me in the eye. "I'm not going to attack you, Finn. I saw the way you were watching me; it was the same way I was watching you. I don't blame you, and I would be lying if I said I didn't think about it. But I don't want to kill you any more than you want to kill me. I know we aren't out of the woods yet, but can we declare a truce? Maybe just for the night? Can you trust me that far?"

"Yes." *I don't see much of an alternative.*

"Good. Thank you. Now, about my little psychotic episode. Ready to talk about it?"

"Sure. It's your story; lead on."

"I want to go upstairs and get some stuff off my desk, okay?"

"Sure. I'll be right here when you get back."

5

When she returned, Mary had a notebook in her hand. "Given my problems with memory lately, I want to refer to this if I need to."

"Sure," I said.

"When I got here, I noticed that a lot of things didn't make sense to me. I decided to get professional help. There's a psychiatrist here who treated me when I was in school. You can probably guess that I didn't have an easy time adjusting to college life, given what you know about my childhood."

"Okay, but — "

"I know. My seeing a shrink is worrisome. Patient privacy only goes so far, but I haven't discussed anything that's criminal with my therapist."

"That's a relief."

"I may be crazy, but I'm not stupid, Finn."

"Of course not. I — "

"Lighten up. I meant for that to be funny. Sorry if it was inappropriate. Crazy is a word that shrinks don't like much."

"I can imagine. But how could that work? Therapy, I mean, when so much of your recent life is off limits?"

"It complicates the process. But that was the advantage of seeing someone I worked with before. We already had boundaries established. I haven't done anything since I've worked with Phorcys that I didn't do before. Over the years, we worked out code words for things I did that I couldn't talk about because they might be crimes. As my shrink said, it's not ideal, but it was the best I could do.

"Anyway, about my problem." She put the notebook on the coffee table in front of us. "I don't think I'll need the notes, but I might. I haven't discussed any of this except with my therapist. And there's nothing in the notebook that will cause any security problems."

"I figured as much."

"I'll cut to the chase here, Finn, but then you can ask me anything you want. The diagnosis of 'brief psychotic disorder' isn't a perfect fit, but it was the best my therapist could come up with. We think my break with reality was drug-induced by whatever they shot me up with in Charleston when Lavrov's thugs snatched me. Otherwise, there was nothing that happened to me that hasn't happened before. I mean as far as a triggering event.

"I didn't share all my background with the shrink, like I said. The trauma of being drugged and kidnapped *could* trigger the disorder that I experienced, and everything else fits. A 'BPD' is by definition — "

"BPD?" I asked.

"Sorry. Spend enough time with these screwballs and you start to sound like them. BPD is short for brief psychotic disorder. BPD lasts from one day to one month, by definition. It's always a short-term thing. If it drags out longer, it's probably schizophrenia. BPD usually fixes itself, although therapy helps speed things along. Therapy helps you avoid freaking out wondering what happened to you. It helps you adjust to having briefly lost your mind, I guess.

"It's rare, so they don't know a lot about it. It doesn't reoccur often, but there are exceptions. Given all the trauma I experienced in my childhood and teens, my therapist thinks this was triggered by the drug they shot me up with, rather than the kidnapping itself. Otherwise, I would have had episodes before now, given all the stuff that's happened to me. The likelihood of relapse in my case is nil, according to the shrink. Otherwise, I would already be living in a rubber room. With me so far?"

"Yes, I think so."

"Do I hear a question lurking in there?"

"Maybe. You make it sound like it's all over, this BPD thing."

"Yes. It was probably all over by the time I got here and hooked up with my therapist, as best we can tell. Except that I was confused and disoriented. We've been working on reconstructing how I got into this mess. I've already told you a lot of my memories of being snatched are fuzzy and disjointed. We were working up to my trying to get in touch with you, so you could help me put them in order, and here you showed up on my doorstep."

"Why didn't you call me, or get in touch through the email drop?"

"I would have, soon."

"I mean earlier? Like right after you figured out what happened?"

"My therapist didn't think I was ready yet. I was in a fragile state, mentally. It's hard to describe what it's like when your whole life comes unstuck. As close as I can come is those bumper stickers that say, 'Shit Happens.' It just does, and in a steady stream. It's scary when nothing in your world makes sense. It's only in the last few days that the therapist thought I was ready, and I've been dragging my feet, because ... "

"Because?"

"Because I knew I was in trouble with Phorcys, for one thing. And I knew you would be caught in the middle, and that I hurt you. I didn't know how to deal with any of those things. Can't you see?"

"I think so. I can't imagine what it was like for you, but I know it can't have been easy."

"You have more questions?"

I shook my head. "I'm sure I will. I don't know where to start, right now."

"Where are we, Finn? I mean, as far as your mission for Phorcys?"

"I need to digest this, and I need to talk to them, obviously. I suspect we'll want our own psychiatrist to examine you, too. Not that I doubt what you've told me."

"Phorcys has a psychiatrist?"

"I'm sure they do, and it will be someone with whom you won't need to establish boundaries, as you put it. In my old job, I went through periodic psychiatric evaluations. It comes with the territory. People like us, we're a scarce resource, and what we do takes a toll on us. Having an in-house therapist is a way of protecting the investment they've made in us."

"But what about the security aspect?"

"That's above my pay grade, but I suspect you and I can both guess the answer to that."

"Where does that leave you and me, Finn? I mean for right now, tonight?"

"We have a truce."

"Yes. But you said you couldn't leave me on my own."

"It's not just me, Mary. Sorry, Kathy. I'll get used to it."

"Oh, don't worry about it. Mary's okay, just as long as nobody else is around. I like the way you say it."

"Okay. But about leaving you on your own — I have a responsibility to make sure we don't lose you again."

"I'm not going anywhere," she said. "I've missed you so much."

"And I've missed you."

"Well," she said, "I don't know about you, but I'm exhausted. It's bedtime."

"Go ahead. I'll fetch my stuff from the car and be right back."

"There's only one bed here. We'll have to share."

"I'll be fine on this couch."

"No you won't. Our truce only goes so far, sailor."

"But what about Sam?" I asked.

She gave me that smile of hers — the one that sends my blood pressure through the roof. "I'll deal with Sam tomorrow. Go get your stuff and hurry back. Top of the stairs and first door on your left. Lock the front door and put the chain on when you come back in."

She stood and walked to the staircase, turning to blow me a kiss over her shoulder as I let myself out the front door.

"Yes, ma'am. I'll be right up."

On my way to my car, I kept looking over my shoulder, watching her townhouse. I knew from my earlier reconnaissance that there was no way for her to sneak out the back.

6

DISORIENTED WHEN I WOKE UP, I DIDN'T RECOGNIZE THE ROOM I was in. Although I was alone in a queen-size bed, there was ample evidence that I didn't sleep alone. Not sure where I was, I scanned my surroundings with caution. Moving only my eyes, I spotted several telltale articles of women's clothing strewn about, but I was by myself. An open door offered a glimpse into an attached bathroom, but it was in shadow. There were no lights on in there. Next to the bathroom door, double sliding doors opened into what must be a closet.

Sitting up, I caught a whiff of coffee. The scent reminded me of waking up on *Island Girl* when Mary was aboard. She often got up first and made coffee as a treat for me. Then it came to me; I was at Mary's townhouse in Gainesville, Florida.

Along with the aroma of the coffee, I could smell bacon frying. I got out of bed and retrieved my clothes, dressing in a hurry. I stepped out of the bedroom into a short hallway and followed my nose down the stairs to the kitchen.

"Good morning, sailor," Mary said. She turned toward me and handed me a mug of steaming black coffee. "Rest well?"

"I did, thanks." I pulled a barstool up to the island in the kitchen and watched her cooking. "How long have you been awake?"

"Not long. I didn't want to disturb you; you were sleeping like you were exhausted — really out of it."

"Best night's sleep I've had since we were in Charleston."

"Yeah?" she asked.

"Yeah. It's nice to be back with you, even if you're Kathy now."

"Oh, stop it, Finn. I told you, Mary's fine, except when we're around other people."

"There's nobody else here, is there?"

"Just us, for now."

"For now? You expecting somebody?"

"Sam will be here in a half hour."

"Should I make myself scarce?"

She smiled. "No, just behave yourself. Be cool; no macho posturing, okay?"

"Not me."

"Good. How would you like your eggs?"

"Any way that suits you will be great."

"Two? Or three?" she asked.

"You cooking grits in that pot?"

"Yes. With a little cheese and heavy cream."

"Two eggs, then."

She nodded. "Two it is. Sorry I couldn't pick up a few fresh flying fish off the deck to go with them. I checked. Nothing on the deck outside but a few geckos; not enough meat on them to be worth the effort. We'll just have to make do with bacon."

I smiled, remembering the first time I served her flying fish for breakfast. "It smells grand. I'll cope."

"What's on your agenda today, Finn?"

"I need to check in with Phorcys, but first I have to work out what to tell them."

"Surely you're going to tell them the truth; you mustn't try to cover for me."

"Cover for you?" I frowned at her. "How could I cover for you, even if I were inclined to? They know most of the story already. And what's to cover? I haven't heard anything that you need to hide, unless there's something you haven't told me."

"I don't want you to spin things to make me look better than I am, Finn. I wouldn't put you in that position."

"That's not what I meant, Mary. What I want to do is present the facts in a coherent sequence, not a disjointed jumble. That's all."

She gave me a rueful smile. "Yeah. *That's all.* That's a handful, isn't it?"

When I didn't respond right away, she said, "I mean, given my mental state — where I started from. A disjointed jumble just about describes my grasp of things, doesn't it?"

"Don't be so hard on yourself. It's too late now, but we should have tried to find out what they used to dope you up. It was something that scrambled your memory; there are plenty of drugs that could bring on a psychotic episode. Even I know that."

"That's what the shrink said, too. Should you talk with her before you call in? Do you have time?"

"I'll make time. Can we do that later this morning?"

"Yes. It should be simple enough, with me there to okay it. She even suggested it the last time we spoke — for a different reason, but still ... "

"Good," I said. "You've done a fair job of laying it all out for me already. Sure, there are gaps in your recollection, but it all hangs together pretty well. With a little help from her, I should be able to give them a solid report."

She put two plates on the island and pulled up a stool. "You're feeling okay about me, then?"

"Yes. But we all know I'm biased."

"Biased, maybe, but not much," she said, loading her fork with scrambled eggs.

"Why do you say that?"

She paused with the forkful of eggs halfway to her mouth. "Less than twelve hours ago, we were talking about whether you might have to kill me. That didn't sound like a man blinded by love. Or even lust." She winked at me, but her face was serious.

"You know how that works, Mary. You're professional to the core. I'm the same way. Whatever else you might have done, I've never seen you put your personal interests ahead of your professional responsibility."

"That's not so, Finn. I wish it were, but I flipped out and wasted those 12 people. How do you square that with 'professional to the core?'"

"We've already beaten that dead horse. The operative phrase is 'flipped out.' I don't see what you did as a conscious choice on your part. After what you've told me, I think that was your psychosis at work. Lavrov's troops provoked your breakdown with whatever they shot you up with, and they damn well paid for it. You may need help to let that go; that's one place that a Phorcys shrink might help you where your normal one can't."

"Thanks, Finn. Your confidence in me helps a lot. You're the only one I can talk with who has even an inkling of what it's like." She looked over her shoulder, glancing at the digital clock on the microwave. "Eat up; Sam should be here any minute."

I nodded and made short work of my breakfast. Mary poured more coffee for each of us and started another pot.

"For when Sam gets here," she said.

We drank our coffee in comfortable silence. That was one of the best things about Mary. I haven't run across many people who find peace in silent company. She feels the same way about me; we've talked about it several times.

The coffee machine chimed. Mary got up and decanted the fresh pot into a thermal carafe. She put it on a tray with three clean mugs and cream and sugar. Lifting the tray, she took it into the living room. When she came back to the kitchen, she looked at the clock again and frowned.

"Sam's never late," she said, picking up her cellphone.

She scrolled through the directory and placed a call, holding the phone to her ear and frowning.

"Voicemail," she said. "Something's wrong. Come with me to Sam's?"

I took a last swallow of coffee and stood up. "You driving? Or am I?"

"I know the way," she said, grabbing her purse and opening a door that led through a small utility area.

I followed her past a washer and dryer. She opened another door, and we entered her garage. A nondescript, midsize Toyota beeped as she pressed a button on the key fob. The clunk of the remote door locks was audible in the quiet of the garage. As I walked around the car and got in the front passenger seat, she touched a switch on the wall and the garage door rolled up overhead.

She backed the car out and closed the garage door. Our

trip was short; ten minutes later, we pulled into the parking lot of a small office park.

"Oh, crap," Mary said, as she parked the car and set the brake. "That's Sam's office."

She pointed down the parking lot to a cluster of police cars, their lights flashing. A news van with a satellite dish on its roof was parked about halfway to where the police cars sat.

"What does Sam do?" I asked.

Mary looked at me, frowning. "Sam's my therapist, Finn. Let's go see what's happening."

7

SOON, WE WERE MINGLING WITH THE SMALL CROWD OF onlookers hovering near the news van. There were 15 or 20 people milling around, held back from the one-story office building by crime scene tape. A bored-looking uniformed policeman kept an eye on us. He lifted the tape for three people in white coveralls who approached from a police van — forensics technicians, I figured. They signed in on the clipboard held by the bored patrolman and entered the building through a glass door.

We were close enough so that when the door swung open, I could make out the lettering on the glass. "Samantha G. Peterson, M.D., Board Certified in Psychiatry and Neurology."

"Excuse me," Mary said, edging away from me, getting closer to a man standing near us.

Tinkering with a big video camera on a tripod, he looked up at Mary's interruption. His eyes flicked over her body and came to rest on her face. He smiled.

"Yes?"

"What's going on?" she asked, smiling back at him.

He glanced at his wristwatch before he answered. "That's a psychiatrist's office," he said, inclining his head toward Sam's office building. "The receptionist came to work and found the door broken into. She went in, 'cause the alarm wasn't going off. Thought her boss probably already turned it off. They weren't supposed to be open yet, but the shrink comes in early most days. So she called out to her. Then this guy hit her over the head. Knocked her out for a few minutes, I guess. When she came to, she went into the shrink's office and found her tied to her chair, unconscious and bloody. That's when she called the cops, and that's all we know. Sorry, but I gotta get another memory card in this thing and get it formatted. We're going live in a couple of minutes."

"Thanks," Mary said.

"No problem." The camera man handed her a business card. "Second number's my cell. Give me a call and we'll go for drinks this evening."

"Great," Mary said, beaming at him. "I'll see you later."

She came back to my side. "You catch all that?" she asked, in a soft voice.

"Yeah. Let's get out of here."

"But ... Yeah, okay." She took my hand, and we walked back to her car.

"Nothing you can do here," I said, once we were buckled in.

"Right," she said, starting the car and backing out of the parking place.

"Where are you going?"

"Back to the townhouse. Why?"

"That's not a good idea," I said. "You know how I feel about coincidences."

Stopping for a traffic light, she turned to look at me, her brow wrinkled. "You think the attack on Sam has something to do with me?" she asked.

"Good chance," I said. "We found you. No reason to think Lavrov would be far behind."

"But how, Finn? And why Sam?"

"Lavrov was working with O'Hanlon, and probably with the Daileys. Either way, the Daileys knew you were a Florida grad, right? You told me that."

"I told them when I was trying to get a job with them, yes. I suppose they might have told O'Hanlon. You think that's enough for Lavrov to pick up my trail?"

"It was enough for Aaron. He was already zeroing in on Kathleen Riley before he found out from your uncle's private eye that you used that name when you were in school here."

"What should we do?" she asked.

"Let's go check out your townhouse, but from a distance. I parked my rental car in that big apartment complex down the way — the one on the other side of the street. It gave me a decent view of your place."

"I know the complex you mean. You thinking of a stakeout?"

"Yes. And maybe skipping out, depending on what we see. Is there stuff in your place that you need? Or can you walk away?"

"You know me, Finn. I can always walk away. But what about your duffle bag?"

"There's nothing in there of any value — just shaving gear and a change of clothes. Everything else is in another duffle bag I left in the SUV."

"Do you think we should disappear?" she asked.

"Not just yet, but I wanted to know if that was an option. I do think we should stake out your place for a while, though."

"I'm okay with either choice, but one thing bothers me."

"What's that?"

"If they're looking for me, how did they end up with Sam? That seems like the long way around."

"Yes, it does. But you said you were seeing her while you were in school, right?"

"Yes. I saw her off and on for several years, but I didn't advertise it. How would they know?"

"She knew you as Kathleen Riley?"

"Yes, that's right. But why would they have gone to her? I keep coming back to that."

"Looking for your address."

"The townhouse ... I see. She knows where I live."

"Right. It took a lot of effort for Aaron to figure that out — the shell corporations, nothing in your name. Different people leasing it over the years — even now, it shows up as leased to somebody else."

"Yes. I'm surprised he got through that. How did he do it?"

"Hacked into your student records; there was a time when you used that address, just briefly. It was the only address you used back then that wasn't a straight-out rental, or a dorm. And the people who leased it over the years turned out to be nonexistent, or most of them did. Even so, we weren't sure. We watched the place for several days. One of his people spotted you — couldn't make a positive identification, but it was a possible. So I came here and knocked on your door."

"Okay, but I'm still puzzled about how they found Sam, and how they connected her to me. If they did."

"I don't know. Let's save that for later. Maybe I'm just being paranoid and what happened to Sam isn't connected to you.

See the silver SUV over there?" I asked, as she pulled into the parking lot where I left my rental car yesterday.

"Yours?"

"Yes. Take the place on the other side of it. That'll give us a view of your place. I'll walk over and take a closer look."

"Wait, Finn. I've got concealed security cameras. Let's see what's been going on."

She took out her smartphone and opened the web browser. Leaning on the car's center console, she held the phone so that we could both see it.

"The one above the door is active anytime the door is open or when somebody rings the bell — or knocks."

She touched an icon and a grainy color photo filled the screen. The time stamp was 25 minutes earlier, while we were in the crowd outside Sam's office.

"Bingo! They don't look too unusual, but I've never seen either one around the place. They don't live there."

We studied the two men, one standing behind the other. They were facing the camera. "They're facing the door in this shot," she said. After a few seconds, she asked, "Okay?"

"Yes."

She scrolled to the next picture, which showed the door open and the two men entering. "This camera's behind them, pointed at the front door. It's triggered when the door opens. So he picked the lock, in less than 30 seconds," she said, pointing at the time stamp.

"What kind of lock?" I asked.

"A good deadbolt, plus the regular one in the doorknob. He knew what he was doing; that's for sure."

"Can you tell if they're still inside? And what they're doing?"

"That depends on where they are and whether they're talking. There's a camera in the garage, and one on the staircase. Other than that, I just have audio inside the place." She tried scrolling again. "The one with the goatee went up the stairs, but he came right back down. He wasn't up there long enough to do more than make sure nobody was home. No more pictures after he went back downstairs, so they're still in there. They would have tripped either the cameras on the door or the one in the garage if they left."

"Try the audio," I said, as she tapped an icon at the bottom of the screen.

There were four icons on the screen now, labeled Living, Kitchen, BR1, BR2. She tapped the one labeled Living, and we heard a man with a whiney southern accent ask, "How long we gonna wait, then?"

"Dunno," the other one said. His voice was gruff — deeper, but no more pleasant. "She shoulda been here. Shrink said she was gonna meet her here, and that woulda been an hour ago."

"Huh," Whiney said. "Who knew shrinks made house calls?"

"Did you check the garage while I was upstairs?" Gruff asked.

"Uh-uh. Forgot," Whiney said.

"Dumb shit," Gruff said.

A few seconds later, a grainy, poorly lit picture of the inside of the garage popped onto the screen of Mary's phone.

"Car's gone," Gruff said.

"You gonna call Sergei?" Whiney asked.

"Not yet, man. Settle down, would you? You're makin' me nervous, all that pacin'. Sit your skinny ass down and be still."

"I don't like it," Whiney said. "Somethin' ain't right. She shoulda been here, waitin' for the shrink. You sure we got the right place?"

"Yeah. This is the place the shrink said. Now shut up, would ya?"

"What do you think we should do?" Mary asked setting the phone aside.

"I'm thinking about that," I said. "You have any ideas?"

"Yes, but I'm doing my best to restrain myself. After Charleston, I'm having second thoughts about killing people, unless my life's in danger."

"Uh-huh. Good for you. We could do it, but think of the aftermath. We'd have two bodies to deal with. And what would it accomplish? Lavrov's got plenty more soldiers. All it would do is confirm that they found you. We wouldn't learn anything from those two."

"But it really pisses me off, Finn. Those shitheads are sitting in my living room, and they hurt Sam, besides."

"They should pay for that, I agree. But there are other ways to collect on their debt to society. There's no need to get our hands dirty on this one."

"What are you saying?"

"Do you have a burner phone?" I asked.

"In the glove box. Why?"

"Call 911. Tell them you just saw two guys break into your unit, but just give them the unit number. Don't say it's yours. Tell 'em you were walking your dog past the front porch, or something. And say you heard them talking about killing some doctor named Sam Peterson. Tell 'em to hurry. Then hang up and strip the phone."

Mary laughed. "Give me the phone, Finn."

I reached in the glove box and passed her the throwaway cellphone. She made the call and delivered her message, disconnecting as the 911 dispatcher told her to stay on the line.

With no wasted motion, she took the back off the phone and removed the battery and the SIM card.

"Now what?" she asked.

"Sit back and watch the show," I said. "Then we'll get out of here."

8

THE POLICE WERE QUICK; WITHIN TEN MINUTES AFTER MARY called 911, there were two patrol cars and a SWAT team in the parking lot in front of her townhouse. They broke the door down and entered. No more than ten minutes later, they dragged the two miscreants out and took them away.

"What's going to happen to my condo?" Mary asked, as we watched the police haul the two confused thugs away.

Now that the action was over, most of the police were gone. There were two plainclothes officers still inside, and two patrolmen in uniform hanging around out front.

"Is there a property manager on site?" I asked.

"Yes. Should I call her?"

"No, not now. It's better if you stay out of it. The police will find her when they can't locate you. Once they're through, I'm sure the manager will take steps to get your door secured. Did the manager know you were staying there?"

"I'm not sure. I didn't check in with her when I got here, or anything like that, so she probably didn't. There's a local realtor here who looks after the place when I'm away," Mary said. "If she knows I'm going to be gone for a while, she arranges short-term rentals, like for visiting faculty — that kind of thing. The manager knows her; that's who she'll call when she can't reach me."

"Sounds perfect, then," I said. "The police will search the unit and try to figure out how to find you. They'll lose interest in you and the condo, eventually. They'll probably charge those two with breaking and entering, but I wouldn't bet that will go anywhere. Once the cops realize they've got the men who attacked Sam and her receptionist, they'll be too busy with that to worry about you. After it quiets down, you can come back and smooth things over."

"What about Sam? I hope she's all right. I feel bad for her, like I should go check up on her."

"That's not a good idea for either of you. Not right now. We should get away from here. It won't be too long before Lavrov figures out his boys messed up; then he'll send reinforcements. Let's head for south Florida. We'll figure out where we're going later, but we shouldn't hang around this neighborhood."

"Okay, sounds good to me. But can I find out about Sam?"

"Sure. Once we're on our way, I'll call Aaron and check in. He'll be able to find out about her, and what the cops are up to. What's the deal on this car?"

"It's registered to the same shell company that owns the townhouse. It's part of the short-term rental package. Why?"

"We'll be better off with my rental car, then. We'll leave this one here and Aaron can get somebody to pick it up in an hour or two. Once the dust clears, they can put it back in your garage."

"Then we might as well hit the road," Mary said. "Grab the other burner phone from the glove box, but leave the registration. I've got an overnight bag in the trunk. I'll take that, and we're ready. What about the keys?"

"Leave them under the mat and lock the car with that electronic key fob. Aaron's people can figure it out, no sweat."

"Really? They'll break a window, or what?"

"No. They have access to a code database, like the car dealers use. They'll read the VIN number through the windshield and program their own key fob. Only takes them a minute — no kidding. A minute, or less."

"Learn something new every day," Mary said, as she stuck the ignition key under the carpet on the driver's side.

She popped the trunk and got out. I unlocked the rental car while she got her overnight bag from the trunk and locked her car. She tossed her bag in the trunk, and I handed her my keys.

"You drive. I'll call Aaron. Before I call him, though, tell me how you found Sam to begin with."

She nodded and got in the car. Before she started it, she asked, "How I found her? You mean how I came to be her patient?"

"Yes."

"Well, I've told you about my, uh ... unconventional adolescence. I was a confused mess by the time I was halfway through my freshman year of college. I needed help, especially after ... well, after my first few contracts. Those weren't my first kills, but before that, I never killed anybody in cold blood. You know what I mean?"

"I think so," I said.

"*You think so*? After all the people you've killed?"

"I suspect it was different for me, Mary."

"Different? How?"

"I've never killed *except* in cold blood. I had to get past my inhibitions before I even got started."

"Never? Really? You must have run into situations where you had to waste somebody you weren't expecting to kill."

"Sure. Collateral damage, and sometimes self-defense. But never in anger, or for personal vengeance."

"Huh," Mary said. "I see what you mean, maybe. Before I took those first contracts, I only killed people who pissed me off. Not that they didn't have it coming; I didn't feel bad about them. It was different after I got hooked up with my agent and turned pro." She paused, a faraway look on her face.

"How did that happen? You've never told me?"

"I got a call one day, out of the blue. It was not long after I wasted this jerk who tried to rape me when I was on the street a few years earlier. You know, when I was a kid. I bumped into him on campus. He didn't remember me at first, but I recognized him straight away. Anyway, it was right after I did him. This woman called me, wanted to meet me. She claimed she could offer me lucrative part-time work that wouldn't interfere with school. I thought she wanted me to turn tricks, or get into the sugar-baby game. You know, long-term escort work. Something like that. I told her I wasn't interested in going back into that world, and she said it was something else. It went from there."

"You said you never met her."

"Yeah, that's right. I met a proxy. I would guess she was a lawyer; she was careful with her words like one, anyway. She never said anything that could get either of us in trouble, but she let me know that they knew about several of my victims.

"After she explained that there might be a way I could make a lot of money by using my *talent* to make the world a better place, I got interested. Money was a big motivator for me back then; I knew all about not having any. She told me to be patient, think about what we had talked about, and watch my email for a few weeks.

"I got a few anonymous emails after that. Every one was from a different bogus address. There was a name, and a photograph sometimes. Sometimes a city. Enough so I could check out the person. They were all nasty characters; it wasn't hard to learn a little about them online. And then I made the connection that a few days after I got an email, each one of them was killed.

"After several of those, I got an email that said, 'Want in?'"

"And you said yes."

"I said yes. A few hours later, I got an email with a name and a photograph. It had one more word than the other emails — 'Yours?' I answered, 'Maybe, if it's worth my while.' I didn't hear anything until the next day. Then I got an email from another anonymous address. '100K. 50 now, 50 later. Details follow.'

"I got an overnight letter the next morning with information about an offshore account in a name I didn't know. I called the bank and gave them the codes from the letter. There was $50,000 there, awaiting my instructions. And that's how it worked. After the third or fourth hit, I got a follow-up call from the proxy. We met, and she asked if I was feeling okay about my life."

"Why?" I asked.

"She said it wasn't unusual for people in my situation to feel a little confused, even depressed, maybe. I didn't say anything, and she said, 'If you ever do, call Dr. Sam Peterson. She handed me Sam's card. We recommend her; she's a psychiatrist. She's good, and she's discreet. But if you do use her, be careful not to tell her anything that she would have to

report to the police. Read these articles before you see her.'
And she gave me another card with references to several articles on doctor/patient privilege. I was struggling with my
conscience by then, and Sam was right in Gainesville, so I
started seeing her regularly. She did me a world of good.
Besides the guilt about the hits, I had all that stuff from my
childhood to work through. After a couple of years, I quit
seeing her, except just occasionally. Until after Charleston,
that is."

"Do you know how to get in touch with that woman? The
proxy?"

"No. Why?"

"I'm trying to figure out how Lavrov got to Sam."

"We don't know for sure that he did, Finn."

"Who else would have tortured Sam to get your address?"

"You're right, I guess. I just don't want to admit it. And that
guy with the whiney voice mentioned Sergei. That sounds
Russian. Maybe that's Lavrov's *Spetsnaz* friend. I'm just
resisting the notion that I brought this down on Sam. She's
such a gentle soul."

"You may be the reason they went after Sam," I said, "but
it's not your fault they found her. There had to be something
else that led them to her."

"Why do you think that? Aaron found me without going
through Sam."

"Yes. But Aaron has some advantages that Lavrov doesn't.
Like access to those reports from the private detective your
uncle hired back when he was looking for you after your
mother died."

"But you said he was already suspicious of Kathleen Riley
before he got those."

"Suspicious, but not certain."

"How did he get that far?"

"I don't know. It's what Aaron does. He has access to all kinds of secure, super-secret government databases. And private ones, as well."

"But how? Phorcys isn't the government."

"I don't know, Mary. We knew you were in school here, and about when that was. We had pictures of you; we knew about your part-time business. Aaron's got hackers working for him like you wouldn't believe, and almost unlimited computer power. Plus, he and his people aren't constrained by red tape — no need for warrants, or permission. And Aaron's got inside info from all those years he was working for the DoD. I'm sure Lavrov's good, but he doesn't have Aaron's connections."

"Okay. I guess we might as well get on the road. I'll take I-75 South for a while. You figure once you talk with Aaron, we'll know where we're going?"

"Yes," I said, taking my encrypted phone from my pocket and scrolling to Aaron's number.

9

"WHAT'S NEW, FINN? YOU FIND HER?" AARON ASKED, WHEN HE answered my call.

"Yes. I'm with her now."

"Put her on the speaker."

"All right, but let me know if there's too much background noise. We're on the road."

I switched the phone to speaker mode, and Mary said, "Hello, Aaron."

"Hi, Mary. We've missed you."

"Yeah. I'll let Finn tell you about it. I need to pay attention to my driving. Traffic's heavy."

"Where are you?" Aaron asked.

"We're leaving Gainesville, headed for I-75 South," I said. "Beyond that, we don't have plans."

"What's going on?" Aaron asked.

"I should start at the beginning," I said. "You got time?"

"Yeah, sure. Should I see if I can get Mike and Bob on the line? Save you doing this twice?"

"You might as well, yes."

"Hold on, then."

"I'm worried, Finn," Mary said, as we waited.

"Try not to be. It'll come out all right."

"But what if — "

"Finn? Mary?" Aaron came back on the line.

"Yes," we said, in chorus.

"Bob? Mike?" Aaron asked.

"Yes," Mike Killington said.

"Welcome back, Mary," Bob Lawson said.

Mary swallowed hard. "Thanks, Bob. You sure that welcome's not premature?"

"Yes. We've already talked that over. Finn wouldn't have made this call with you on the line if things weren't all right."

Mary looked at me, her face pale, her eyes big and round.

I muted the microphone on my phone. "Take a deep breath and drive. Trust me. You'll come through this okay."

When I switched the microphone back on, Mary said, "Thanks. I'm driving, so Finn's going to explain."

"You're up, Finn," Mike said. "Fill us in."

"Okay. Here's the overview. Whatever it was they shot Mary up with when they snatched her in Charleston, coupled with the trauma of it all, caused a breakdown. She lost her bearings, knew she was in trouble, and headed for Gainesville. She's been in the care of a psychiatrist here who treated her back when she was a student, and she's recovered, mostly."

"In a month?" Mike asked. "I'd think you would need to be in therapy longer, Mary."

"The diagnosis was a brief psychotic disorder," I said. "Typically lasts anywhere from a day to a month, I'm told. But there's more, and that's why we're on the run."

"You're on the run?" Mike asked. "Why? Somebody's after you?"

I gave them a brief version of everything that happened this morning. "Given that Lavrov's probably behind this morning's events, we thought it would be best to hit the road."

"That sounds like the right decision," Mike said. "You have a destination in mind?"

"No, but we're headed south," I said. "I figured somewhere in the Miami area, for a start. Also, I'm hoping you can fix Mary up with an in-house shrink. Mary's therapist was pushing her to sit down with me and start putting everything back together. And her doc didn't know what we do for a living. It would be good if you can find somebody like we used to have back when I worked for the government."

"You're in luck on that one," Bob said. "We just brought Jill Hardwick on board. You remember her, Finn?"

"Yes. She's the one I was thinking of. That's perfect. How are we going to make this happen?"

"Aaron," Mike asked, "is the lodge usable?"

"Yes. The renovations are all finished. But there's no staff."

"That should be all right. For this, we're better off without staff. Finn and Mary and Jill can fend for themselves. Can you get somebody to stock the pantry and get three of the cabins ready for occupancy by tonight?"

"I can do that."

"Good," Mike said. "Bob and I will brief Jill and have her meet the three of you there. You don't need to stay once everybody's settled, Aaron. Or you can; suit yourself."

"I'll stay the night, anyway," Aaron said. "I can play it by ear from there."

"Anything else?" Mike asked.

"I have some things I want Aaron to chase down," I said. "Otherwise, nothing else."

"Okay, I'm going to drop off," Mike said. "Mary, welcome back. We were worried about you. I'll be in touch."

"Thanks, Mike," Mary said.

"Yes, thanks," I said.

There was a click as Mike disconnected, and then Bob spoke. "I'm glad you're back with us, Mary. But I never doubted that you would be. Finish getting well; we've got a backlog of work for the two of you."

"Sorry if I've held things up," Mary said. "I wouldn't have been of much use, the shape I was in."

"Understood. We'll talk again soon, you and I. Goodbye for now." Bob disconnected.

"Okay," Aaron said. "I've got my work cut out to get the lodge ready. What do you need?"

"We want to know how Lavrov found Sam Peterson," I said. "I didn't go into all the details with Mike and Bob. Mary had trouble coping with her new career after she turned pro a few years ago. Her broker recommended Peterson as somebody who could help. They trusted her, but they cautioned against sharing anything the doctor would be obligated to report to law enforcement."

"Okay. That's enough to get me started. Maybe this evening you can fill in some blanks if need be. Anything else?"

"Yes. I want to know how Sam's doing," Mary said.

"All right. That should be simple enough. I'll want to find out what the police are up to; we need to make sure this is Lavrov's work. Their files will tell us what you want to know, I'm sure. If not, we'll hack the hospital's system. What else?"

"That's it from our end," I said. "But where is this lodge?"

"I'll send you a text with a map and GPS coordinates; that's the only way you'll ever find it. What kind of car are you driving?"

"A rental," I said. "Why?"

"What kind of rental?"

"A silver Nissan SUV. Why?"

"The last few miles are unimproved dirt road through the swamp. I'm not sure how a standard sedan would fare, but you should be fine with an SUV. See you this evening."

"Bye, Aaron," Mary said.

"Drive carefully, you two." And with that, Aaron was gone.

"What do you think?" I asked, putting the phone in the center console.

"They *seemed* to take it in stride," Mary said. "But I know I'm not out of the woods, yet."

"Nobody's ever out of the woods with Mike and Bob," I said. "Comes with the territory."

"You know what I mean, Finn. I felt somebody walking over my grave when Bob said that."

"Said what?"

"'Finn wouldn't have made this call with you on the line if things weren't all right.'"

She turned and looked at me briefly, her face going pale again. Looking back at the road, she swallowed hard.

"Don't let that upset you. You're reading more into it than — "

"No, Finn. You're trying to make me feel better, and I appreciate that. But I need to keep in mind that I'm only alive because you three think I can be redeemed."

"Don't get yourself worked up over this, Mary. I made my decision about you yesterday when you leveled with me about Charleston."

"That's just great, Finn," she said, in a sharp tone. "What more could a girl want? The man I love tells me he decided to let me live for a while longer. It doesn't get much better than that."

"Mary, it wasn't like that. You're — "

"It was like that. Don't make it worse by trying to sugarcoat it. And don't tell me how I should feel about it, either. I'm the one who determines how I feel. I understand the position you're in, you and Bob and Mike. If I'm off the rails, I'm a big liability to you. That doesn't mean I'm comfortable with it. It's scary as hell."

"What do you want me to say?"

"Nothing. I want you to listen to me; you're the only one I can talk to."

"Okay. Even though I'm scary?"

"*You're* not scary. It's this whole mess that's scary. I know what you are; you and I are more alike than different. I can't know what it would be like to be put in the position you were in. But if our roles were reversed and I were told to decide whether to take you out, I can guess how I would feel. A big part of me would be heartbroken, but that wouldn't stop me from killing you if it were necessary. Is that where you are?"

"Not any longer, but yes. That's an accurate enough picture of where I was."

"That's so awful, Finn. For you to be put in that position, I mean. And it's my fault. I'm so sorry."

"It's not your fault, Mary. You didn't choose to get shot up with some drug that induced psychosis. Blame Lavrov. He's the one who put us in this situation."

"I was careless enough to let them — "

"Let it go, Mary."

She gripped her lower lip between her teeth, focusing on the traffic, not saying anything. After a few minutes, she said, "Okay. I'm in control. I've got a grip on myself. Thanks for putting up with me. Guess I'm still a basket case. But I will get better. I promise."

"I believe you. You're one tough lady. Scary, even."

She flicked her eyes toward me for a quick look. Deciding I wasn't mocking her, she asked. "Scary, huh? Really?"

"Really. I've seen what you can do when you're mad."

"Mad's the right word," she said. "And I don't mean angry. What I did to those people in Charleston? That was madness at work."

"'Out, out, damned spot ... '" I said.

She took her hands off the wheel for a moment, pretending to wash them. Returning her left hand to the wheel, she held her right under her nose, sniffing it. "'Here's the smell of the blood still. All the perfumes of Arabia will not sweeten this little hand,'" she said.

"You know Macbeth. Act V, Scene I, anyway," I said.

"I told you once before that I minored in theater. Of course I know Macbeth. I even understudied the role of Lady Macbeth for a campus production. I'm surprised you placed my response, though. And why did you toss out that clichéd line, anyway? Everybody's heard that one, but most people don't know where it comes from."

"It fits. Your madness reaches beyond the killing, just like Lady Macbeth's. I keep telling you, Lavrov and his people put you in that position. You shouldn't ... oops. I was about to tell you how to feel, again."

"It's okay. Finish your thought."

"Their blood may literally be on your hands, but at the risk of provoking you, I would say you weren't in control when you killed the people aboard *Anastasia*."

"I'm working on that, still," she said. "I understand the logic, but accepting that I wasn't responsible for my actions isn't easy. It means I have to admit that I'm not always in control of what I do; that's difficult for me."

"I can understand that. And you couldn't go into detail about that with Sam, could you?"

"No. That was awkward. She and I both knew there was something I wasn't telling her. That must have frustrated her, but she never let it show. I gather you know this Jill Hardwick. Is that right?"

"Yes. I told you I went through periodic psychiatric evaluations when I worked for the government. She was our in-house shrink."

"Really? There were enough people like you to justify having an in-house psychiatrist?"

"I never knew how many people like me there were, but this is the government we're talking about, Mary. Efficiency wasn't a big deal; secrecy was. And she worked with others in the group besides the front-line troops like me. She spent a lot of her time consulting with the intelligence group — Aaron's people. I know he used her to predict the behavior of targets."

"You've discussed kills with her, then? Your kills, I mean?"

"Yes. Every one of them, at some point along the way."

"She was there that long?"

"Yes. My first session with her was when I joined the group."

"She must be old, then."

"I don't know, but I'd guess she's in her late 50s, maybe a little older. Rumor was she came from the CIA. She's been around."

"Will I get along with her okay?"

"I'm sure you will; she's easy to talk to. That's her job, remember?"

"Okay. I wonder when Aaron will know something about Sam. I hope she's okay."

"I'm sure he'll call us as soon as he has anything. Or we'll see him in a few hours. Let me know when you need a break from driving."

10

"THIS PLACE REALLY IS IN THE BACK OF BEYOND," I SAID, AS Aaron opened Mary's car door. We were parked in a small clearing in the undergrowth, but we were still under a canopy of cypress trees.

"Have any trouble finding it?" he asked.

"Not with your directions. But now I see why you didn't just give us the GPS coordinates."

He laughed as he helped Mary out of the car. "I'm Aaron Sanchez," he said, as he released her hand. "It's nice to meet you in person, finally."

"Thanks, and yes, it is nice to put a face with your voice. Finn's right. GPS coordinates wouldn't have gotten us through the swamp. What is this place, besides hard to find?"

"You'll see," Aaron said with a chuckle. "Grab your gear and follow me."

Mary and I got our duffle bags from the back of the SUV, and Aaron led us along a poorly marked trail through the undergrowth that surrounded us.

"It's no accident that it's hard to find. We've got another 100 yards along this footpath. In the early 1900s, a bunch of rich guys built the lodge as a getaway, a place where they could come and misbehave with no repercussions. It was a club, I guess, but maybe not that formal. There's still plenty of game, and the fishing's out of this world. We're on the northwest edge of the Everglades, as you probably figured. This is private land. And here we are."

We left the path as we came into an area clear of undergrowth. There were several wood-frame, one-story structures. The largest, in the center of the clearing, was the size of a small single-family home. The others appeared to be one-room cabins. Aaron led us onto the porch of the largest building.

"Welcome to the lodge," he said. "This is the main building; there's a kitchen and a dining room, plus a lounge area. The cabins are for sleeping, and they have basic plumbing, since our renovation. There's another building farther back in the sticks. In the old days, it was a dormitory for the hired help. There hasn't been a decision yet as to whether we'll staff this place, but my guess is not. Mike's thinking maybe a caretaker who'll live on the premises — retired military, no doubt. But the idea is that the fewer people who know about the place, the better it'll serve our needs."

"But aren't there records of the purchase, or something?" Mary asked.

"No. The property's been in Mike's family for generations. It's owned by an obscure, family-controlled trust. Until we renovated them, the buildings were rotting away and overgrown. You could have walked past them a few feet away and not noticed them. And you've seen how hard it is to get here."

"How about by water?" I asked.

"We're a few miles from Dismal Key, up at the north end of

Chokoloskee Bay," Aaron said. "You could hike in from a boat, if you were determined enough and the gators weren't hungry. It's tough going, though, and there's no straight-line path. You'd be breaking trail the whole way."

"What about utilities?" Mary asked.

Aaron laughed. "We're seriously off the grid. We've got a solar array a good distance from here. It's disguised as a fake cellphone tower. There's a battery bank and inverters there, with underground cable to bring AC power into the lodge and the cabins. Fresh water comes from a cistern. But we do have cellular service. It doesn't seem like it, but we aren't very far from civilization, as the buzzard flies."

"I didn't see your car," I said.

"No. I caught a ride out with the provisions. We try to keep the vehicle traffic down. Speaking of that, did you have any trouble with the road?"

"No," Mary said. "But I engaged four-wheel drive. I think it would be hard for a regular car. You were right about that."

"Yeah. That's by design. It's getting on toward dinner time. Why don't you drop your stuff in that first cabin and come on back here? I'll rustle up something to eat."

"Good enough," I said. "See you in a few minutes."

Mary and I stepped down from the porch and walked to the nearest of the cabins. We found the accommodations clean and comfortable, but basic. We went back to the main lodge and let ourselves in. Aaron was working in the kitchen.

"What's for dinner?" Mary asked. "Smells good."

"Our special tonight's prime rib *au jus*, with roasted mixed vegetables. It'll be ready in about ten minutes. Help yourself to beer or wine from the fridge behind the bar. Or there's an assortment of liquor in the cabinets."

"Where'd you learn to cook?" I asked.

Aaron laughed. "I didn't. But we've laid in a supply of prepared meals from a yacht provisioning operation. They're pretty good for dinner. You'll find them in the freezer. This refrigerator's stocked with cold cuts, plus bacon, eggs, and sausage. Oh, and salad makings, too."

"Where's Jill Hardwick?" Mary asked.

"She's arriving in the morning. Her preference is to meet with you alone, to begin with. She wants to get acquainted with you without either of us in the way. I have some stuff to cover with Finn, anyway, while you're talking with her. And I have some information on Samantha Peterson and that whole Gainesville situation. You want to get into that while dinner heats up?"

"Sure," Mary said. "Mostly, I'm worried about Sam."

Aaron nodded. "The prognosis is guarded. She was beaten severely; two fingers broken. She hasn't regained consciousness yet, so they're being cautious. There's no skull fracture, no sign of a dangerous head injury. But she's definitely got a serious concussion. The receptionist is okay. She's gone home. She was only out for a couple of minutes, as best they can figure."

"Bastards," Mary said. "Any word on how they found out she was treating me?"

"Those two were just muscle. They're clueless. They were told to make her tell them where to find you; they said they were supposed to hold you and call in for further instructions."

"Call in?" I asked. "Who were they supposed to call?"

"They wouldn't say. And now they're all lawyered up, but that probably doesn't matter. They're known associates of a big-time drug dealer in Jacksonville. They're street soldiers, though. There would be a few layers of insulation between them and the boss man, so they probably don't know much beyond what the cops got from them already."

"Who's the boss man, then?" I asked.

"David Grissom."

"Is he one of O'Hanlon's bunch?" Mary asked.

"Well, here's where it gets interesting," Aaron said. "He's not on the list. It seems like he worked for James Stringfellow until a couple of months ago. Remember that name?"

Mary frowned. "It sounds familiar, but no, I can't place him."

"Savannah," I said. "Before we got the word to back off, he was our next target after Charleston."

"Oh, right!" Mary said. "I remember now. So Grissom worked for Stringfellow, but he runs things in Jacksonville?"

"Both of those statements are true," Aaron said, "But it's doubtful that he still works for Stringfellow. We think he got promoted. O'Hanlon's man in Jacksonville was Joe Waters, but he was killed shortly before Grissom showed up in Jacksonville. And get this: Waters was found sitting behind the desk in his home office, with every bone in his body broken."

"*Zamochit*," Mary said. "Lavrov and his *Spetsnaz* goon?"

"That would be my bet," Aaron said.

There was a pinging sound from the oven timer. Aaron put his beer down and opened the oven door.

"Dinner is served. Can we talk about something else while we eat?"

"Sure," I said. "Tell us about the fishing around here. You said it was good."

11

We sat at the breakfast table, talking. Tired from our drive yesterday, Mary and I turned in early last night, right after our dinner with Aaron. We met him at the lodge this morning. While we were eating, Aaron gave Mary a new Phorcys-supplied iPhone with a custom operating system to replace the one she lost.

Finished with breakfast, we lingered over coffee, killing time until Aaron heard from Jill Hardwick. When she called, she announced that she was entering the dirt road through the swamp. Aaron and I left Mary in the lodge to wait for Jill while we took the trail out to where we left my rental SUV.

"Will we wait for Jill to get here before we take off?" I asked. "The road's too narrow for us to pass her on our way out."

Aaron and I were going to a quick meeting with Mike and Bob. According to Aaron, they wanted a few minutes with me outside Mary's hearing. Besides, Jill Hardwick wanted Mary to herself for their first day's counseling session.

Aaron chuckled at my question. "No. She's coming in by a different route. There are several ways to get through the swamp. We wanted to make sure that our comings and goings wouldn't be easy to observe, so we rotate the use of the routes. Jill will park in another spot and take a different trail. She may already be introducing herself to Mary."

"I see," I said, as we got in the SUV. "Where to?" I asked, as Aaron buckled his seatbelt.

"Make your way back to the Tamiami Trail and head for Marco Island. We've got a safe house there. Mike and Bob should be there about the time we get there."

"What's on tap after we meet them? We've got the day to kill, right?"

"I'll be surprised if they don't have some suggestions for you on how to spend your time while Jill works with Mary."

"Speaking of Jill," I said, "how did she come to join us?"

"Once you killed Nora and Lavrov got her boss, our old group fell apart. There was nobody left except the worker-bees. Then you killed the Secretary, and there was nobody left who even knew Nora's little group existed."

Aaron and I worked for Nora; her boss was an undersecretary reporting to the Secretary of Defense. We were there for about 20 years before we left and became part of Phorcys. We discovered our whole chain of command was corrupt. Before we left, we did some cleanup work, and then we parted ways with them. Part of our cleanup was getting rid of Nora, but that's another story.

"So you and Mike and Bob have been doing a little recruiting?"

"Sort of. Let's just say the sharper people found their way to us. The ones who had a good handle on what was going on. That would be Jill and a few of my key people from the intel group."

"What will happen to the others?"

"I'm not sure. The other field operatives won't have a problem finding work, and the inside troops will get absorbed into the bureaucracy without much trouble."

"How many of them know what happened, do you think?" I asked.

"Only the field operatives would have a clue — Nora's direct reports. The others who were left were so compartmentalized they have no idea what the group was even doing."

"The field operatives are the ones who worry me," I said.

"Yeah. Don't lose sleep over it. We're on top of them. There weren't many, and most of them have been picked up by other agencies already. You know what those people are like; they've got their own connections, just like you and I do."

"What if some of them go astray? Or go into business for themselves?"

"So far, none of them has. But if that happens, we'll take care of it. We know who they are, and there's not one who's a match for you and Mary. If we need to, we'll take them out."

"Speaking of Mary, do you have a reading on where Mike and Bob come out on her?" I asked.

"As far as I know, that's up to you and Jill. You're the one with the most at stake; they trust your judgment."

"What about you?"

"What do you mean, Finn?"

"You've been busy digging into everything there is to know about her, Aaron. I know you; you would've done that whether or not Bob and Mike ordered it. She's pulled the wool over my eyes before; I'm being cautious. I want to know if you've found anything that's inconsistent with her story — her recent story, or her ancient history. If I have to make the call on her, I want to know as much as there is to know."

"Yeah, I hear you. There's nothing that sticks out. We

haven't been able to backtrack from that one killing she told you about — the one that brought her to the attention of her 'broker,' as Mary refers to the woman. All we know about that is what she told you earlier. She probably killed a few lowlifes before she got him, but nobody that attracted any attention. The one she told you about the other night got a lot of publicity, but nothing that tied back to her."

"What kind of publicity?"

"He was a rich kid. A campus cop found him with his pants around his ankles in his Mercedes roadster in a spot near the edge of the campus that was favored for late-night trysts. He was gagged, his hands bound to the steering wheel with duct tape. Kneecapped and sexually mutilated. Left there to bleed out, which didn't take too long, according to the coroner's report." Aaron paused and looked over at me.

"Ugly," I said. "No evidence to point to a killer?"

"No. The rounds in his knees were hollow-points fired at close range — contact shots. The bullets were too fragmented to yield any usable ballistic markings. The guess was nine-millimeter, but that's about it. The cutting was done with an extremely sharp knife — nice, clean wounds. And the victim was no angel. Several women accused him of sexual assault over the years, but none of them would testify. Speculation was they were either intimidated or paid off to keep them quiet. Or both, in a couple of cases."

"No wonder that got the broker's attention."

"Yeah. There was a lot of press coverage. The kid's father was a high-roller, a big operator in politics at the state level. A money man. He made sure all the relatives of his son's accusers were thoroughly investigated. The case is still open — unsolved."

"Sounds like he got what was coming to him," I said.

"Yeah. That was the sentiment in the opinion pieces in the press. Still, it was a vicious piece of work. And well done, too. But to answer your question, that's the first time we could pick up Mary's trail, other than what was in the private detective's report on her that Bob gave us. And we would have never connected her to that hit, except for what she told you the other night."

"Are you sure she did it?"

"Well, that's a good question. The short answer is no, but given what she told you, it's highly likely that she did. The timing fits perfectly with the beginning of her odd travels back in her student days. Plus, it wasn't too long after that that she began to show evidence of a big change in her finances. Nothing too flashy, mind you, but enough of a change to support the story that she found work. And that's about all I know, except the stuff she did for Phorcys before you and I joined. I hope that makes you feel better about her."

"It does. Thanks."

"Glad I could help. Pull into that subdivision up there on the left. We want the sixth house on the right, on the main road."

12

THE HOUSE WAS IN AN UPSCALE DEVELOPMENT. THE HOMES weren't overwhelming, but this was an expensive neighborhood. Upper middle class, but nothing too flashy. There was an ordinary-looking SUV in the semicircular driveway.

"That's Bob's car," Aaron said, pointing at the SUV. "Just pull in behind it."

Pulling up close to Bob's vehicle, I got out and stretched the kinks out of my back. When Aaron slammed his door, I locked the car with the remote, and we walked up to the entrance. I rang the bell, and Mike opened the door.

"Come in, gentlemen," Mike said. "Bob and I are in the den; there's coffee and juice if you'd like."

He motioned for us to go through an archway, and Bob greeted us as we entered the living room. "Good morning. Make yourselves comfortable. Need a break from the road or anything?"

"Morning, Bob, Mike," I said. "I'm okay for now."

"Same here," Aaron said.

"Good," Mike said. "Have a seat and let's get started. Jill sent us a text a few minutes ago; she and Mary are settling in with one another. Finn, now that you're away from her, what do you think?"

That was Mike; no beating around the bush for him. "I think she's okay. Still struggling to put the pieces in order — her memory of what happened before Charleston was scrambled, but it's coming back. I couldn't tell how far back in time her confusion went. But then I didn't know her all that long before Charleston. She's also annoyed with herself for losing control, as she puts it."

"Losing control?" Bob asked. "What does she mean by that?"

"She's upset that she flipped out and killed the people on *Anastasia*. She says it was a temper tantrum; it didn't meet her self-imposed standards of professionalism."

"Uh-huh," Bob said, with a nod. "Her psychotic break could explain that, according to Jill. I'm surprised her own therapist didn't help her figure that out."

"She held back a lot of information from Dr. Peterson; Mary didn't want to put her in an ethical bind."

"I'm not sure I see the logic there," Bob said. "I think telling a shrink about past crimes is protected. It's telling them about crimes you plan to commit that's a problem."

I shrugged. "I can only go by what Mary told me. When her broker's people hooked her up with Peterson, they warned her about what she could say safely. Maybe they were overly cautious, or maybe she misunderstood."

"From what Jill told us, the drugs and the shock of being snatched off the street would have been enough to set Mary off," Mike said. "And she said the shock of Mary's coming to grips with killing the crew on Lavrov's yacht would have added to her problems. Do you see anything that argues against that view?"

"No," I said. "Unless Jill comes up with something we haven't thought of, I think Mary's playing straight with us."

"What's your take on whether we can put her back to work?"

"I'm comfortable with her loyalty. What worries me is the effect it will have on Mary if we ask her to kill again. I'd like Jill's opinion on that."

"Right," Bob said. "Same here. We already asked Jill about it. Her answer was guarded, as you'd expect. But she says that if Mary's break was indeed triggered by the drugs, she'll probably be okay. She needs to deal with her feelings about the temper tantrum, but other than that, Jill says the prognosis is good — pending her first-hand examination, of course."

"Jill's other comment was something about not waiting too long to get back on the horse," Mike said. "If Mary's psychotic break was really what we think, then she'll be okay to return to duty once she sorts out her confusion. Probably the sooner the better. Jill says she's either done for good, or she'll be okay soon. Jill will know more in a few days. How do you feel about that? Trust Mary to have your back, still?"

"Yes. My gut reaction is that if Mary's in the heat of battle, her instincts will win out over this new-found doubt of hers. After all, that's what happened on *Anastasia*; her instincts took over."

"Good," Mike said. "We'll see where Jill comes out. Now, let's talk about you."

I looked at Mike, feeling my brow wrinkle as I wondered about his shift in direction. "About me?"

"Yes," Bob said. "We need to know how you feel about going back to work while Jill's counseling Mary."

I relaxed. "Thanks for asking, but I've been doing this almost as long as Mary has been alive. Nothing's changed as far as I'm concerned."

"You sure about that?" Mike asked. "We know how close you two are."

"Yes. My feelings for Mary aren't tangled up in what I do for a living, Mike. I appreciate your concern, but I've told Aaron before, it's like there are two different people inside me. I learned to isolate my work from my personal life a long time ago."

Mike smiled. "I knew you'd say that, but we both wanted to hear it. And Bob and I know what you mean. We've been there."

I nodded, waiting to see where he and Bob were going with this.

"We've made a decision on Lavrov," Mike said. "Before Charleston, we wanted to watch him and learn more about him, but we've changed our position. He's too dangerous; we have to take him down. First, though, we have to find him. We'll make him the next target for you and Mary, once she's got Jill's blessing."

"Okay," I said. "If I'm right about Mary, she'll like that. No matter what she says, she's extra pissed off at Lavrov after Charleston. Getting even with him will appeal to her. Just my uneducated opinion, you understand."

Mike and Bob laughed.

"What's funny?" I asked.

"Your uneducated opinion, my ass," Mike said. "You're a shrewd judge of people. Save that 'aw, shucks' routine for somebody who doesn't know you."

"Well, I — "

"Hey, Finn?" Bob asked.

"Yes?"

"We've got an idea on how to draw Lavrov out into the open. Let's kick that around. We're spinning our wheels talking about Mary until Jill gets through with her."

"Okay," I said. "What's your idea?"

"The police are still holding those two men who attacked Dr. Peterson. We're thinking about starting the rumor that they're cooperating. That there's a secret federal task force that's going to roll up their whole chain of command, including David Grissom and whoever he's working for."

"How's that going to get Lavrov out in the open?" I asked. "Seems like it would have the opposite effect."

"Well, if that's all we did, it probably wouldn't flush him out. But we have in mind some sleight of hand that will make him think more of his direct reports are cooperating. He'll have to respond to the threat; if it's broad enough, he may be forced out in the open. Besides Grissom, we're thinking about Stringfellow and Theroux. Remember them?"

"Savannah and Charleston," I said. "Mary and I were staking out Theroux when she was snatched in Charleston."

"Yes," Bob said. "We thought Lavrov killed Theroux, but the body in Theroux's office turned out to be someone else's."

"But based on what we know about Lavrov's methods," I said, "when they met him, they were blindfolded. They can't identify him, so why will Lavrov see them as threats?"

"We've been thinking about something Mary suggested, back before she was kidnapped," Mike said. "Remember when Lavrov left her that voicemail pretending he wanted to recruit her as his enforcer?"

"Yes. What about it?" I asked.

"She wanted to send him a text to provoke him, get him off balance," Bob said. "Or maybe even take him up on it and go undercover in his organization."

"I remember. She was hoping we could make him stumble somehow and give himself away. We were still thinking that over when his people snatched her."

"Right," Mike said. "We've decided we like that idea."

"Wait," I said. "We thought that was too dangerous for her back then. It's even more dangerous now."

"It was her idea of actually going undercover with him that was too dangerous," Mike said. "Provoking Lavrov won't make him any more dangerous than he already is."

"But isn't it a little late for Mary to send him a text responding to his voicemail? That was over a month ago."

"Yes, probably so," Bob said. "We have a different provocation in mind. We'll plant the rumor about that bogus federal task force, and then we will make Stringfellow, Theroux, and Grissom disappear. We want to make it look like they're being held somewhere. Then we'll do the same with his guy in Miami."

"You want us to kidnap them?" I asked.

"No. That's too much trouble. Just kill them, but leave no sign. No bodies, no evidence of what happened." Mike said. "Then Aaron's people will run a disinformation campaign to make it appear that the four of them are in custody somewhere."

"Wait," I said. "That won't fly. If they were under arrest, they would be entitled to lawyers; they wouldn't be invisible."

"Only if the government were following the rule of law," Mike said. "But they aren't — not these days. That's why we're here."

"Granted," I said. "But I still don't see how this would work."

"Think about the government rhetoric these days, equating the war on drugs to the war on terror," Aaron said, breaking his long silence.

"Okay," I said. "So you plan to put out the word that they're terrorists. How does that change things?"

"Guantanamo," Aaron said, "or better yet, a mysterious black site that nobody knows about."

"But these guys are U.S. citizens," I said. "The government can't treat them that way. Lavrov's smart enough to know that."

"Correction," Aaron said. "The law doesn't allow the government to treat them that way. But our current government isn't playing by the rules. Picture what will happen once these four disappear in the middle of the night and the word leaks out that they're being held incommunicado. No lawyers, nobody even knows where they are, because they're such dangerous terrorists. And that they're being interrogated under duress."

"The liberal establishment will be all over it," I said. "They'll be standing in line at the courthouses to file lawsuits."

Aaron grinned. "Most likely. The government will deny everything, but nobody believes what they say any more. Their denials will just reinforce the bogus story."

"Talk about 'fake news,'" I said.

"Hey, they're the ones who coined that phrase," Aaron said. "We're just showing them how to play the game they invented."

"Okay," I said. "This will make the government look like a bunch of thugs again. Nothing new there. How's that going to flush out Lavrov?"

"His operation will come to a sudden halt in the southeastern U.S. He'll have a big staffing problem; he'll have to replace four of his key people, his direct reports. Besides that, he's going to turn up the heat on the bureaucrats and politicians who are on his payroll. He'll blame them for letting this happen. Lavrov's no armchair general; he's going to have to show up on the front line, where the action is. And we're determining where the action is, so we'll have you and Mary waiting for him."

"This is starting to make sense," I said. "But why are we starting in Jacksonville?"

"Optics," Mike said. "He sent two guys from Jacksonville after Mary, and they're in custody. We'll treat that as the chink in his armor that allows the government to roll up his operation. Exploit the opening in Jacksonville, and then move on to Savannah, and Charleston, because that's where he started the fight. It will look like we're following a trail given to us by the Jacksonville people. If that doesn't flush him out, we'll crush the Miami operation. By then, he'll be out of business in the southeastern U.S."

"But he's going to be all over the people he's paying for protection," I said.

"Yes," Mike said, "and they will deny everything — like Aaron said, nobody will believe them, especially not Lavrov. They've told too many lies already. Lavrov may even take a few of them out before we get to him — save us the trouble. What do you think?"

"Sounds good to me," I said. "What do you want me to do next?"

"Get yourself up to Jacksonville and figure out how to nail Grissom. Your first task is recon. You've already got a handle on Charleston, so your next stop after Jacksonville will be Savannah. In a week, you should have a plan for how to take the three of them out with no trace. Once you've got the details worked out, we'll know whether Mary's ready, and take it from there. Questions?"

"No," I said. "That's clear enough. If there's nothing else, I'll get on the road to Jacksonville and stake out Grissom beginning tonight."

13

DAVID GRISSOM'S HOUSE — A MANSION IN A COMPOUND, actually — was on the southern edge of Jacksonville. It was one of several similar places in a gated, golf-course community. This was another Dailey development, if I didn't miss my guess.

I infiltrated the gated community as dusk was settling, working my way through the undergrowth that surrounded the golf course. With Grissom's place in sight, I climbed into the lower branches of a big live-oak tree. Settled in a spot high enough to let me see over the undergrowth but low enough not to be screened by the tree's foliage, I took a pair of night-vision binoculars from my backpack. I was less than 100 feet from Grissom's perimeter wall. While surveying his place, I thought about the day's events.

After my meeting with Mike and Bob, I made the five-and-a-half-hour drive to Jacksonville. I stopped at a sporting goods store in the southern suburbs and picked up a few odds and ends for my nighttime stakeout. Checking into a motel on the

Interstate close to Grissom's neighborhood gave me a chance to rest up for my evening's work.

Before I went out for dinner, I called Mary's new encrypted phone, the one Aaron gave her this morning. I was surprised that she answered; I thought she might still be busy with Jill Hardwick.

"Hi, Finn. I hear you're out looking for work. Save some for me, okay?"

"Aaron told you," I said.

"Yes. Not specifically what you were doing; just that Mike and Bob gave you a recon mission. I'm not supposed to ask for details."

"Okay. How's it going with Jill?"

"She's great. You were right; she's easy to talk to. We covered a lot of ground today."

"Any reaction from her yet?"

"Well, she's keeping her assessment to herself, but I think I'm telling her what she needs to hear."

I didn't doubt that for a second, remembering how convincing Mary's tales could be. She led me on more than one merry chase through fabricated stories early in our time together. Jill's ability to sort fact from fiction would be more objective than mine when it came to Mary's stories. Still, I wouldn't bet against Mary's being able to fool her, if that's what Mary wanted to do.

"Sorry," she said, with a laugh. "I just realized how that sounded; that's not what I meant. I'm being honest with her; I want her help. But I'm feeling good about how it's going. She's helping me organize all my tangled feelings about what I did, helping me put things in perspective. I'm glad for the chance to work my way through this with somebody like her. She assured me up front that if I was honest with myself and with her, we would come out in the right place. And the right place will be one that's acceptable to me and to Phorcys, she said. I'm not supposed to worry about what her assessment will be. She says there won't be a conflict between her recommendation and what I want, by the time we finish."

"Are you comfortable with that?" I asked.

"As long as she gets the right answer, I am. I know what I want out of this."

"What's that?"

"The go-ahead to kill Lavrov."

"Suppose you and Jill don't see eye to eye on that?"

"We will, Finn. Count on it; I'm going to keep talking until we do."

"I hope it works out," I said, suppressing a chuckle. This was the Mary that I knew and loved. Her uncertainty and doubt were in the past already. Whatever Jill thought, I knew Mary was ready to go back to work. "I'll need your help before this is over."

"I'm in, sailor. But I'd better go. I'm supposed to have dinner with my Uncle Bob in a few minutes. Call me later?"

"I'm not sure I'll be able to; I've got a night stakeout ahead of me. But we'll talk again soon. I'll at least call you before breakfast in the morning. Glad you're feeling better."

"Thanks. I miss you."

"I miss you, too," I said, and disconnected the call.

14

THERE WAS A MOVEMENT ON THE PATIO BETWEEN GRISSOM'S
house and the lighted swimming pool. Forgetting my memories of the day, I lifted my binoculars. A tall, shapely blonde in
a string bikini strutted out onto the pool deck. She unrolled a
yoga mat, bending over to flatten it out.

Another flicker of motion caught my eye as a man in a robe
stepped out of the house. He was not David Grissom; Aaron
showed me several photographs of Grissom earlier. Too bad I
didn't have a camera with a telephoto lens so I could email a
picture of this guy to Aaron.

Carrying a cocktail in one hand and a fat cigar in the other,
the man settled into a chair at a round table. He put his drink
on the table and the cigar in an ashtray, shifting the chair so he
could watch the show. The girl smiled and blew him a kiss
before she began stretching.

Turning my attention to ways we might breach Grissom's
defenses, I examined the top of the wall around Grissom's
property, looking for signs of intrusion alarms. There were
several fixtures along the wall that could be infrared light

sources, as well as housings for security cameras. Lowering my binoculars, I was reaching into my backpack, feeling for the cheap cellphone I used as an infrared detector. As my fingers closed around it, I felt a sharp, stinging bite on the side of my neck. Thinking it was a wasp, I raised my hand to brush it away, but I felt myself falling. I was drifting off to ...

THE NEXT THING I REMEMBER, I was listening to two men talking. I wasn't sure where I was, so I lay still and kept quiet. I was flat on my back on a hard, cool surface, maybe a concrete floor. My wrists were bound; my arms extended over my head, stretched uncomfortably. Trying to flex them, bending my elbows, I felt immediate resistance; my wrists were anchored to something solid.

Cautiously, I tried to open my eyes, but they were taped over, the lids stuck to the tape. My mouth felt dry and full; it didn't take much movement of my tongue to let me know there was a rough, absorbent piece of cloth crammed in to keep me quiet. Wrinkling my cheeks, I could feel that the rag was taped in place.

My ankles were bound and fastened to something heavy enough to keep my legs extended. I was immobilized, wherever I was. I began trying to focus on what the two men were saying, but I must have drifted off again before I picked up any useful information.

When I regained consciousness again, I was in pain. Not agonizing pain, but I was feeling stiff and sore, my muscles cramping. At that point, I was only vaguely aware that I woke up earlier; it came back to me as I was evaluating my physical condition. Working my way through the sensations from my body, I remembered that I was tied up, gagged, and blind-folded. Then I recalled the men talking. Were they still here?

I started counting off the seconds as I listened. I wasn't sure, but I thought I could hear someone breathing steadily, rhythmically. Maybe there were two of them, still, I thought, as I picked up overlapping rhythms in the breathing. They sounded like they were asleep, but I couldn't be sure. After about three minutes, a telephone rang.

"Shit," a man said, his voice rasping like he was a heavy smoker. "Get that would ya?" He yawned.

"Get it yourself," a second one said, his voice sharp. "You're closer, dumb ass." His tone showed he was accustomed to giving orders to raspy voice.

There was the creaking sound of a heavy man getting out of a chair. The phone was silenced in mid-ring, and raspy voice said, "Yeah?"

A couple of seconds passed, as I pictured him listening to the caller. Then he spoke again.

"No. He's still out cold from the dart."

Another pause.

"I dunno. He's been out since about 9 o'clock last night. That shit can take a while to wear off, Sergei said. Sometimes a whole day."

A second or two of silence, and then, "No, man. Like 24 hours, a whole day. Sergei said even if he woke up before that, he'd be loopy, worthless to question him. We could try to wake him up, I reckon. Want us to?"

Another short interval passed, and he said, "Yeah, sure."

He hung up the phone and said, "Asshole."

"Which asshole was it?" bossy voice asked.

"Dixon."

"What did he say about waking him up?"

"Not to bother," raspy voice said. "Mr. Grissom won't be back until next week. We got plenty of time to mess around with this piece of shit, find out who he is and what he was doing. Dixon said just leave him be until tonight, unless he wakes up. Then we're supposed to call him. He wants to be here when she questions him."

"Yeah? Sick bastard. He gets off on watching her do stuff like that."

"Can't say as I blame him," Raspy said. "She's one hot mama. Her and her damn string bikinis. I wouldn't mind her asking me a few questions."

"You ever seen her question somebody?"

"Uh-uh. Why? What's she do? She got some special tricks?"

"I won't spoil it for you, not if this is your first time. But trust me, if they ever sic her on you, just tell her whatever they want to know and get it over with. Your only hope is to make her mad so maybe she'll kill you quick, instead of the other way. You got something to look forward to tonight, especially if this guy tries to be a hero. If she gives him the full treatment, you'll be sleeping with the lights on for a week. If you can sleep at all after seeing her in action."

"Hell yeah!" Raspy said. "I can't wait, man. You reckon since our boy's out cold for a while yet, we could go get us a little breakfast?"

"Sure," Bossy said. "He's not going anywhere. Bring that backpack he was carrying. I want to try to crack that iPhone of his."

I heard the squeak of upholstery springs. Bossy voice must have been on a sofa. Then there was the sound of a door opening and closing. I was trying to imagine what the bikini babe had in store for me, but the drugs in my system were too strong, I guess.

15

A SOLID KICK TO THE LEFT SIDE OF MY RIBCAGE ROUSED ME.

"Wake up, asshole," Raspy said.

I groaned into my gag.

"Strip him," a woman said. "Cut his clothes off but be careful. When he bleeds, it will be because I want him to. If you so much as scratch him, you get the next turn in the chair. And get that tape off his eyes. I want him to see what's happening."

"But then he'll recognize us," Raspy said.

She laughed, a nice, musical laugh, all the more chilling because it sounded as if she were genuinely amused. "That won't matter, you fool. And that's the last time you will question my instructions. Are you clear on that, sweetheart?"

Raspy said, "I don't — "

"Shut up, dumb ass. Do what she says." The bossy one was here, too.

I felt one of them scratching at the tape over my eyes, and then I yelped into my gag as he ripped off my duct-tape blindfold. A heavy-set man knelt beside me, the tape still dangling from his hand.

"Good boy, Bobby," the woman said. "Now, cut his clothes off, but remember, not a scratch on him or you'll be next after I finish with him."

So the heavy-set man, Bobby, was the hoarse one. I could smell stale tobacco smoke mixed with his body odor. I lifted my head a little and cut my eyes in the direction of the woman's voice. She was the bikini babe, the one doing yoga by the pool last night. She wore a blood-red string bikini that missed being decent by a few millimeters in several critical dimensions. She no doubt thought she radiated sex appeal, but the look on her face was enough to quell any reaction of that sort.

Her eyes were wild, flicking around as she tapped her right foot on the floor with jerky movements. Her fingers were in constant motion, too. She was keeping time to music that only she could hear. I wondered if she was high on something, or just crazy.

Standing next to her was the man who was with her at the pool last night. His arm was around her, his hand on her nearly bare hip in a possessive way. Was he the one with the bossy voice?

"Now, Bobby," she said. "If he's not naked in the next thirty seconds, I'll use you for the opening act." She laughed again, that rich, genuine laugh that was a sure sign she was nuts.

Bobby slipped a knife from the side pocket of his jeans and flicked it open with his thumb. She really got to him; his hand shook as he cut away my clothes. He sliced through the laces of my running shoes and took them and my socks off. Bobby was thorough. When I was stark naked, he rocked back on his heels and looked up at her.

She slapped her companion's hand away from her hip and sashayed over to stand next to Bobby, reaching down with one hand to rub his head. "Good boy," she said. "Maybe I'll have a little treat for you, if you keep it up."

Bobby was practically panting. He grinned up at her. I wondered if his tail was wagging, or if it was tucked between his legs. Probably wagging; he didn't seem very bright.

She blew him a kiss and took a half step back, turning a bit and snapping the pointed toe of her red, high heeled pump squarely into his crotch. "Don't drool when you look at me, you pervert," she said, as he doubled over, dropping his knife as he grasped his wounded parts. She stepped close to him and raked his cheek with the red-lacquered nails of her right hand.

Instead of the scratches I expected to see on his cheek, there were four deep razor cuts, bleeding profusely. She held her hand up, studying her nails, and I could see the bits of a razor blade under each one, held in place by superglue. An old trick, but it surprised poor, dumb Bobby.

He put a hand to his damaged cheek, stroking it, and then looked at his hand to see why it was wet.

"You cut me," he said, his voice more raspy than usual.

"You were looking at me, pervert, stripping me with your eyes. I know what you were thinking. You can't have me, not even in your dreams. But I can have you, any time and any way that I want. Now, both of you, get him in the chair before I lose my patience."

A third man came into my field of view and crouched beside Bobby. Picking up the knife Bobby dropped, he moved away. In a second or two, I felt a jerk on my arms and then the tension eased; he must have cut the rope that held my arms extended. He came into view again, moving toward my feet, and I watched as he sawed through another rope. Trying to move my arms, I found that they were numb; my legs wouldn't move either.

"Okay, asshole," the new man said. "I'm gonna cut your wrists and ankles loose, but don't try nothing stupid."

He was bossy voice. That must mean the man with the bikini babe was Dixon. I could feel Bossy doing something at my ankles, and my feet began to tingle as the circulation to them improved. Keeping still, I followed him with my eyes as he moved back to my wrists and cut through the cord that bound them together.

"Let's stand him up, Bobby," the one with the bossy voice said.

"Okay, Bubba," Bobby said.

Bubba and Bobby. And Dixon. But I still didn't have a name for bikini babe.

"On my count of three," Bubba said, as I felt the two of them gripping me under my arms.

Bubba counted to three, and they lifted me to a vertical position. My arms flopped, useless, and my legs felt like rubber as they dragged me to a sturdy-looking, open-frame commode chair. It looked like something scavenged from a nursing home, except that it was missing the waste receptacle that slid under the seat. It sat squarely in the middle of a heavy vinyl tarp. Next to it, there was a small table on wheels, laden with a selection of gleaming surgical instruments.

Bobby and Bubba turned me around when we were a foot or two from the chair and plopped me down on the seat. Bubba moved behind the chair and held me in an upright position while Bobby cinched a piece of heavy webbing around my midsection. Once I was strapped in, they taped my forearms and wrists securely to the armrests. Dixon and bikini babe watched from a few feet away. She was twitching, licking her lips as Bobby and Bubba spread my knees apart and taped my legs to the legs of the chair.

"Get his head," Bubba said.

Bobby grabbed my hair and pulled my head back against a headrest as Bubba peeled off a strip of duct tape.

"No, you fools," bikini babe said. "Leave his head free for now, so he can watch the fun. And get rid of the gag, so he can answer my questions."

Still holding my head against the headrest with one hand, Bobby used the other to rip off the duct tape over my mouth. "Spit out that rag, asshole," he said.

I was happy to comply.

"Good," bikini babe said. "Now, get out of my way."

Bobby and Bubba hurried to one side as she stepped up in front of the chair. She stood facing me, looking me in the eye. Taking a deep breath, she made a visible effort to relax. Her nervous tics subsided, and she let her eyes roam over my body as she began a series of deep breathing exercises.

"What should I call you?" she asked, after several seconds. Her voice was calm, and she no longer acted high. The effect of her sudden change in demeanor was chilling, as she no doubt meant for it to be.

"Whatever pleases you, ma'am," I said, locking eyes with her.

"Polite, aren't you? That's nice, but it won't help either of us. Did he have ID?" she asked.

"No," Bubba said.

"What did he have with him when you captured him?"

"A backpack," Bubba said. "Couple of bottles of water, some beef jerky. Cheap cellphone, plus an iPhone. Binoculars. Keys to a rental car, and a folding combat knife. Plus a camouflage poncho."

"Did you find the car?"

"No."

"Okay, stud," she said, putting her hands on my arms and leaning toward me, her face almost touching mine.

I felt the headrest against the back of my head as she put her lips on mine. I clenched my teeth and pulled my lips together tightly as I felt her tongue probing. After several unsuccessful attempts to force her tongue into my mouth, she stood up, smiling at me.

"Playing hard to get, are you, big boy?"

She reached toward me and stroked my cheek. Remembering what she did to Bobby, I wasn't surprised when I felt the blood running down the side of my face.

"I'm one of those girls who likes a challenge. Hard to get is what I want from a man. We'll have fun tonight, you and I. I'll take you places you've never been before. You'll feel things you've never even dreamed about, not in your wildest fantasies. And we have all the time in the world, so you just drag it out as long as you want. I like that."

"Sure you don't want to tell me who you are before we become ... uh ... intimate?" She ran her hands over her bare skin, writhing as she licked her lips while maintaining eye contact with me. "You're making me all hot and bothered; I don't want to rush this, though. So maybe I'll just amuse myself with Bobby for a little while. You can watch; will that get you in the mood? Do you like to watch?"

"I'm in your hands," I said.

"Not yet, but before the night's over, you will be. In ways you would never imagine. Bobby and I will give you a preview. How about it, Bobby? Want to play?"

"Uh," Bobby said, swallowing hard.

"Aw, come on. I know you do. I won't hurt you. Not much. Now take off your clothes."

"Um, how about later, after we finish with this guy?"

"Now, Bobby. Bubba?"

"Huh?" Bubba asked, frowning, his hands shaking.

"Give me that knife so I can undress Bobby."

Bubba handed her Bobby's lock-blade knife, the one that he used to cut me free. She opened it with a flick of her wrist and turned to Bobby. Moving in close, she pressed herself against him. The poor fool wrapped his arms around her and began moaning as she writhed in mock passion.

16

BIKINI BABE TOOK HER TIME WITH BOBBY. SHE WAS ENJOYING her warm-up act, as she called it. In periodic asides to those of us in her audience, she would explain what she would do to him next, while we watched Bobby squirming, his eyes rolling in fear. After listening to him scream for the first few minutes of her ministrations, she ordered Bubba to put a ball-gag in his mouth.

"Too bad it's not an apple," she said. "We could roast him like a pig after I gut him."

By that point, Bobby was hog-tied, his wrists and ankles pulled together behind his back as he rested face-to-the-floor on his ample belly. In different circumstances, he might have been pitiful. But not now — I can never find it in me to feel sorry when a wanna-be badass gets a taste of what he serves up to others.

She rolled him onto his side and told Bubba to spin him 90 degrees, so that his so-far uninjured chest and stomach faced toward her audience.

"Or maybe we shouldn't roast him. Look at all that prime

bacon." She ran her hand down his side, from his armpit to his hipbone. The pieces of razor blade glued under her fingernails opened four long cuts that immediately filled with blood.

"Reasonably well marbled," she said. "But fatter would be better. Maybe I should neuter this hog so we can fatten him up before we roast him."

She reached down as if to fondle him with her enhanced nails and then hesitated. Looking back over her shoulder and catching my eye, she smiled and blew me a kiss.

"What do you think, Stud? Ready to tell me your name? I'm getting bored with Bobby. There's not much to work with there. You look a lot more promising. Let's you and me play for a while. How about it?"

"I'm at your disposal, ma'am," I said.

She stood up straight and turned to face me. "You've seen a sample of the things I can do for a man," she said, as she sashayed over to stand between my knees. "Anything in particular that appeals to you?"

"It was all awesome," I said. "I guess it's up to you."

She stroked my other cheek, the one that was still intact, then bent toward me and kissed it. I waited a second, expecting to feel the blood dripping along my jaw, but it didn't happen.

"See," she said. "I don't always use my claws. I can be gentle if you're nice to me."

"I'm glad to hear that, ma'am."

"Let's try kissing again," she said. "But first, tell me your name. I don't like calling you Stud; it sounds too much like I'm treating you like a sex object."

She put her hand on my good cheek again, but she kept it in one place, curling her fingers a bit, letting me feel the bits of razor blade. "Tell me your name."

"Finn."

"Finn," she said. "Is that your first name, or your last name?"

"Everybody just calls me Finn."

"Okay, Finn. How about that kiss, lover boy?"

"I'm ready if you ... Wait a second."

"Why, Finn? Wait for what? You're making me hot, baby."

"I don't even know your name."

She laughed, that perfectly normal, spine chilling laugh of hers. "I like you, Finn. Call me Carmen."

"You don't look like a Carmen."

"No? What do you think I look like? You want to give me a name? I can be anybody you want me to be. Tell me."

"Maybe we should stick with Carmen. It's starting to sound — "

There was a coughing sound from the left, and she staggered to her right as the right side of her head exploded. She collapsed in a heap between my feet. I tried to turn my head far enough to see the shooter, but I couldn't.

Dixon and Bubba jumped to their feet. There were more coughs, and Bubba fell back into his chair, a small black hole at the bridge of his nose. Dixon was on the floor, screaming.

"Shut this bastard up while I cut Finn loose," Mary said.

"You got it," I heard Aaron's voice say, as something muffled Dixon's screams.

"Are you okay?" Mary asked, as she sliced through the bonds that held me to the commode chair.

"Better by the minute. How did you — "

"I'll tell you later. I want to talk to the one I kneecapped and then we need to clean up and get out of here. Can you stand up?"

"Not sure," I said, grasping the arms of the chair and trying to rise. "Legs are still numb from being tied up so long. Arms, too."

"Well, you work on that while I see what this jerk knows." She moved away, and I turned far enough to see her rip away the duct-tape gag that Aaron had applied to Dixon's mouth.

Dixon gasped for air and started to scream again. She kicked him hard in the belly; his scream was cut off.

"Scream again and I'll blow out your elbow," Mary said. "I know it hurts, but you're a tough guy, and it won't be for long."

I saw that both his knees were shattered, bleeding profusely as he watched Mary.

"Aaron's with you?"

"Yes. He's sorting out a few bodies we left on our way in. Now, you focus on getting your arms and legs working while I interrogate this one."

"Dixon," I said.

"What?" she asked.

"His name's Dixon. He's in charge here."

"That much we learned from the guards we caught."

She rested a foot on one of Dixon's damaged knees. "Where's Grissom?" she asked.

"I have no — "

Mary put weight on her foot, and he screamed again. "Don't waste my time, Dixon. And stop that screaming. It just makes me want to hurt you more. Believe me, there are things I can do to you that are more painful than stepping on your knee."

"Please, I don't know — No! Don't! I'll tell you everything."

I stood up, holding onto the chair. Turning, I saw that Mary held a combat knife, its point barely penetrating the skin of his lower left eyelid.

"Give me any more bullshit, and I'll cut your eye out,

slowly. And remember, you've got another one to lose. I'm in a hurry. Start talking."

"Okay, okay. Grissom's at some kind of meeting in the Bahamas. There's this Russian guy he answers to, and they're all there. But I don't know where, exactly. He's gonna be gone for several more days. He's due back next week. They — "

"They, who," Mary asked. "You said they were all there, at this meeting. Who all is there?"

"The others who work for the Russian. I don't know all of them, just the ones Grissom works with. There's a guy named Theroux, from Charleston, and — "

"I already know their names. Did you work for Joe Waters before Grissom?"

"Yeah."

"Who killed Waters?"

"This guy named Sergei. He works for the Russian. Maybe they were in the Army together; they've known each other a long time."

"Sergei, huh? Another Russian?"

"Yeah. He's like the enforcer."

"Does he have a last name?"

"I don't know what it is."

"Were you there when he killed Waters?"

"Yeah. He made us all watch."

"Us? Who?"

"Me and Sylvie and Bobby and Bubba. Everybody who worked for Joe. He and his buddy, they tied us all up, and his buddy was gonna zap us with a taser if we even blinked. Sergei broke all of Joe's bones, starting with his toes, and then his fingers, and he — "

"We already know that. Was the one you keep calling the Russian there?"

"No. Nobody ever sees him. When Joe went to meet him the first time, Sergei and his buddy blindfolded him. Same with Grissom."

"Does Sergei's buddy have a name?"

"Not that any of us ever heard. And they only speak Russian to one another. I guess, Russian. That's what Grissom said it was."

"The one you keep calling the Russian — does he have a name?"

"Uri Lavrov is what Grissom said, but he doesn't think it's his real name."

"I think you're lying about where Grissom is," Mary said.

Dixon screamed as she jerked the knife up. She slapped him, hard, across his face.

"Tell me where he is, or I'll take the other eye."

"I d-don't know, honest! I'd tell you if I — "

"Okay, enough. I believe you." Mary's pistol coughed after she interrupted him.

17

"HOW'RE THE LEGS, FINN? THINK YOU CAN WALK OUT OF HERE?"

"Yes. Where's Aaron?"

"He's going to sanitize this place before he leaves, make it look like a rival drug lord did this. Your rental car still around? Or did they take it?"

"Bubba said they couldn't find it, but they took my key. And my backpack."

"I've got all your stuff. It's right outside the door. Which one's Bubba?"

I pointed to his body. "The one that's all trussed up is Bobby; he's still alive, I think."

"Not for long. Aaron will take care of him. Put these on. We need to get moving."

She handed me a shopping bag containing a pair of jeans, a polo shirt, underwear, socks and running shoes. "Thanks," I said, once I was decent again.

"Your face is all bloody. You okay?"

"For now. It's just cosmetic; it was about to get a lot worse."

"I'll clean you up when we get to the car. Let's get out of here."

"I'm with you; lead the way. How did you find me?" I asked, as Mary led me through a maze of corridors and out into the night.

"Your phone. I got worried when you didn't call me this morning, so Aaron enabled the tracking on it."

"This morning? I've lost track. How long have I been here?"

"They caught you last night, sometime. Can you find where you left your car?"

"Yes. It's in a state park campground about two miles from here. I hiked in across the golf course. I was in the woods, up a tree overlooking the pool; I can find our way from there."

"This way," she said, following a driveway through an open gate.

We passed a beat-up Humvee on our way out, and I saw that the two halves of the gate were mangled.

"Stay with me, Finn. We'll follow the wall. This is the front entrance; the pool's in the back. How are you holding up?"

"I'm okay. The longer I walk, the better I feel. They shot me with a dart, some kind of drug. I overheard them say it would take 24 hours to wear off. I must be getting close."

"Could be. We don't know exactly when they caught you."

"Not too long after dark," I said.

"Then your 24 hours is about up."

"I'm surprised Aaron came with you. Did Jill give you the all clear?"

"Aaron and I decided to come after you. Jill was a little doubtful about it."

"How about Mike and Bob?"

"They were out of touch when we left the lodge, but we talked to them later. They were okay with it, I guess."

"You guess?"

"Aaron and I didn't give them much choice. He's awfully loyal to you. He told me he wouldn't be alive except for you."

"Yeah. I'm not sure why he keeps saying that. He would have been okay."

"That's not the way he sees it."

"I know. I'm still surprised he came with you. I didn't know he did field work these days."

"He doesn't, but given my recent problems and what we heard from Dixon and company, he thought I might need a hand getting you out. He really didn't want to turn me loose on my own, I could tell. But he kept that to himself."

"What do you mean by what you heard from Dixon?"

"Aaron didn't tell us everything about the phones he gave us," Mary said. "Once I raised the alarm with him, we went to his place. Have you seen it?"

"No, never."

"He's got all kinds of stuff there."

"Stuff?"

"High-tech gear, and some odd characters working for him, too. Hackers. Anyway, he has remote access to these phones. We used your phone to eavesdrop on Dixon and his minions. They were in a room with your backpack, where they went through what you were carrying when they caught you."

"I'll be damned. That pisses me off. He's been listening in on me all this time."

"Get over it, Finn. It saved your hide. Sylvie planned to make designer handbags out of you."

"Sylvie? That's the bikini babe?"

"Yes. Dixon's girlfriend. She was one sick woman. Disgusting, too."

"Disgusting?"

"I don't want to talk about it. But she had the hots for you, 'Stud.'"

I swallowed hard. "Thanks for saving me. So how much did you hear?"

"Not a lot. We listened in long enough to hear that they captured you, and that Dixon told them not to question you until tonight, when the drugs wore off. Then we had to hit the road to get here in time. Once we left Aaron's, we couldn't eavesdrop. That equipment's not portable."

"You cut it pretty fine, as it was," I said.

"Oh, we were in control of the house before they started interrogating you. Once Sylvie decided to make an example of Bobby to soften you up, Aaron left me to keep an eye on things while he searched the house."

"Keep an eye on things? How?"

"I was in their security control room. This place is really something. They have motion sensors and night-vision cameras all through the area. There's a perimeter that's maybe 200 yards out from the wall where they can see everything that moves. That's probably how they found you to begin with.

"Plus, that room you were in was wired. It's like a recording studio, for audio and video. Soundproofed and everything. I had a ringside seat; full color video and high-fidelity sound of what Sylvie was doing to the one named Bobby. There were a bunch of recordings of her other sessions, too."

"I'll be damned."

"Maybe so, but not tonight. You still doing okay?"

"Yes." We were well into the undergrowth, now. "We're about ten minutes from the car."

"You just left it in a campground? Weren't you worried the management might notice?"

"It's a state park; you pay on the honor system by dropping

an envelope in a box. I set up a tent and left some stuff around to make it look like I was out fishing."

"Where did you get a tent?"

"I stopped at a sporting goods place on my way here."

"Clever," Mary said.

"Not clever enough. I walked into a trap."

"Lighten up, Finn. Remember what you told me. You can't control everything all the time."

"I made an amateur's mistake. I'd be a handbag if it weren't for you and Aaron."

"Several handbags. But an amateur wouldn't have had me and Aaron to save his ass. Now, let it go."

"Easier said than done."

"Tell me about it. Maybe Jill can do a group session for the two of us."

"Are we going back to the lodge, then?"

"Yes. Aaron was already starting to narrow the search for Lavrov down to the southern Exumas before this. Now that we know he's got his direct reports with him for the next few days, I'll bet Mike and Bob will send us after them."

We pushed through the scrub in silence for another few minutes. When we found the car, Mary helped me break camp and pack everything into the SUV. She swabbed my face with a damp paper towel.

"You'll heal. Just a few deep scratches. It looked a lot worse before I washed the blood off. I'll get some ointment at the first place I see. We should keep moving, though."

"You keep saying that. Is somebody chasing us?"

"You never know. They had the keys to this car, remember? The license number is on there. We don't know if they passed it on to somebody before Aaron and I shut them down."

"You said you had the keys," I said.

"Yes, and the rest of your stuff."

She hefted my backpack and tossed it in the SUV. I must still be dopey; I didn't notice that she picked it up before we set out.

"Get in," she said. "I'm driving; I don't ride with druggies, *Stud*."

"Yes, ma'am. But I'm okay. And I didn't like it when she called me Stud."

"That's what they all say. Don't give me any trouble, or I'll put on a string bikini and make a handbag out of you."

"Anything but that, please. I'll do whatever you want."

"I'm going to hold you to that when this is over."

"Yes, ma'am. I hope so."

18

I FELL ASLEEP ONCE MARY GOT US TO THE HIGHWAY. DRUGGED or not, I was still exhausted. When I woke up, we were stopped. Startled, I looked around and saw that we were at a gas station just off the Interstate. Mary was filling the tank. I started to get out of the SUV, but she held up her hand and shook her head. She finished with the pump and got behind the wheel.

"Do you need to go to the restroom?" she asked.

"No, I was just going to stretch my legs."

"Later, then. I just talked to Aaron. We need to keep moving. The feds showed up and surrounded Grissom's place right after Aaron got out of there."

I shook my head. "The feds?"

"That's what he said. He barely missed getting caught inside their perimeter; they've choked off the whole area."

"That's strange," I said. "How did they get there so fast?"

"I don't know, Finn."

"Should we switch cars, or something?"

"We've come almost 150 miles. Aaron figures we're good.

He's about 20 minutes behind us. He says they've got check-points set up on the roads around the gated community, but we're well beyond them."

"How does he know?"

"You're asking me? You're the one who has known him forever. How does Aaron know anything?"

I shook my head. "That's Aaron. How did you get past Grissom's security when you came in to get me?"

"We knew there was no point in stealth. You saw the Humvee, right?"

"Yes," I said.

"Aaron used an antitank weapon; an M72, he called it. He got out and blew the gate apart and I drove the Humvee through. He rushed the door with a 12-gauge pump shotgun with two rifled slugs up front. He took down the door with that and we cleaned out the security detail as we went. Eight of them, besides the people in the room with you. They never knew what hit 'em."

"Is he following us in the Humvee, then?" I asked.

"No. He had some of his people waiting close by. They picked him up. They stole the Humvee from a drug dealer in the area while we were driving up from the lodge."

"They? You mean Aaron's people?"

"Yes," Mary said. "I didn't realize he had so many people that he could call on. And they're spread around, too. This bunch was from Jacksonville."

"I don't know much about his organization, but he never seems to come up short. So the Humvee is part of his misdirection, I guess."

"Yes. He's set it up to look like this was a rival drug dealer out to rob Grissom, or maybe kill him. That's about all I know about it. But Aaron's handy in a gunfight; I'll say that for him."

"He is that," I said. "I can vouch for it myself. You okay, or do you want me to drive for a while?"

"I'm fine. Besides, I'm not about to let you behind the wheel. I remember when I was doped up with whatever they use. I felt wide awake after an hour, but I know better, now."

"Why do you say that?"

"From watching you," she said. "You're loopy. You're drifting in and out on me, flickering on and off like a burned-out neon sign. I know you don't think so, though. I've been there."

"I'm fine, Mary. I had a nice, long nap, until you stopped for gas a few minutes ago."

"Uh-huh." She laughed.

"What's funny?"

"That was an hour and a half ago when we stopped for gas. We're less than an hour from the lodge, now. Go back to sleep; I'll wake you when we get there. Sleep's the best thing for you right now."

I knew better than to argue with her. The last thing I remember about our trip is reclining the power seat.

When Mary shut off the SUV's engine, the silence woke me. Dawn was breaking, although it was gloomy. We were shrouded in patchy fog.

"Morning, sailor. Rise and shine," Mary said, as she shook me gently, her hand on my shoulder. "You doing okay?"

"Uh-huh. Where are we?"

"The lodge. I took the same route in as the first time. Ready for a hot shower?"

"Sure. And I'm starving."

"I'll bet you are. They didn't feed you, did they?"

"Not that I remember. Every time I came to, I was stretched out like I was on a rack; couldn't move a muscle."

"Then you haven't eaten for 30 hours, give or take. Should

we stop in the main building and raid the refrigerator first? Get a little something in your stomach?"

We got out of the SUV and she opened the rear hatch. Grabbing both of our backpacks, she led the way to the trail through the undergrowth.

"Yes," I said, hustling along in her footsteps. "A quick snack sounds good, then a shower and a big breakfast afterward."

"Good. We can do that. It'll give Aaron time to get here."

"Who else is around?" I asked.

"Jill's probably still here. I don't know about Mike and Bob. But it's early; I wouldn't bet anybody's up and around yet." She held the door of the main building for me.

I went straight to the refrigerator. A half-pint of milk and two slices of cheese and salami jammed between slices of bread did wonders for me.

"Now," I said, "about that shower ... "

"Come with me, sailor. I'll take care of you."

Thirty minutes later, I was freshly shaved and wearing clean clothes. Mary was putting antiseptic ointment on my cheek. She used butterfly bandages to close the deeper parts of the cuts.

"I think you'll be good as new, once those heal," she said. "They're not deep; I don't think you'll get any new scars out of this one. That was some manicure your new girlfriend had."

"She had little pieces of a razor blade glued under her nails," I said.

"Yeah, I figured. That's not a new trick; I used to do it myself. A girl has to defend herself."

"It didn't work so well for her," I said.

"No, not that time. Taught her a lesson about fooling around with my man. She needed something a little tougher than razor blades to stop a nine-millimeter round."

"She made a mess out of Bobby, though," I said. "Wonder if there was some history there?"

Mary shrugged. "Hard to know. I think she was just plain crazy, myself. And don't make any smart-ass comments about why I would know that."

"Not me. I'm scared of girls."

"Good. You should be; girls are dangerous. You okay for a few minutes?"

"Yeah. Why?"

"I want a quick shower and fresh clothes myself. Then we'll go cook some eggs and sausage."

"With grits and toast," I said.

"Sure. Give me five minutes."

"Take your time," I said, stretching out on the bed to wait.

Ten minutes later, Mary and I were busy in the kitchen. Aaron showed up before we got everything cooked.

"How're you doing, Finn?" he asked.

"Better by the minute. But Mary says I'm still loopy."

"Yeah, well, more than usual?" Aaron said. "You can't blame everything on drugs, you know. I've known you a long time."

"Thanks, wiseass."

"Yeah. All kidding aside, I'm glad you're back. From what Mary said in her texts, you will be fine — no lasting damage."

"Other than to my ego," I said.

"Give yourself a break," Aaron said.

"Yeah, Finn. I told you to lighten up," Mary said.

I shook my head. "I should have been scanning for infrared sources before I approached that wall. I saw the ones on top of the wall before they got me, but it didn't occur to me they'd be watching the undergrowth that way."

"Not a bad thought," Aaron said. "But it wouldn't have done you any good last night. They were watching the undergrowth, all right, but they weren't using active infrared."

"But Mary said when she was in their control room, she saw that they had cameras covering a swath about 200 yards out from the perimeter wall."

"Yeah. They were using the latest thermal imaging technology. It's passive. That makes it impossible to detect, using anything we know about."

"That's pricey hardware, isn't it?" I asked.

"Yeah. It isn't commercially available. That stuff's classified — still under evaluation by the government."

"Then how the hell did Grissom get his hands on it?"

"That's a good question," Aaron said. "Right up there with how the feds knew to show up right after Mary and I crashed the party."

"Maybe the neighbors complained about the noise when we blew the gate," Mary said.

"Maybe," Aaron said. "These guys weren't responding to a 911 call, though. It wasn't even a normal special ops deployment. They weren't just trying to catch us; they set up a defensive perimeter like they were expecting a follow-up assault. We're talking maybe a hundred people, with heavy weapons."

I frowned. "That sounds odd."

"Yeah. It was the type of response you'd expect if they were defending the White House or something."

"Why would Grissom warrant that kind of protection?" Mary asked.

"I don't know," Aaron said. "I've got feelers out."

"They were too late, anyway," I said. "You were already out of there, from what Mary said. They missed the chance to save Grissom's troops. You think maybe it was Dixon they were trying to protect, instead of Grissom?"

"Could be. They were about 15 minutes behind us. They were responding to our incursion, but I don't think they were trying to save anybody. I think they knew we were gone. They set up their perimeter defense before they even approached the house."

"How do you know that?" I asked.

"We tapped all their surveillance gear, pulled remote feeds so we could see what happened after we left."

"Are you still getting the feeds?" I asked.

"No. They eventually shut everything down. But as best we can tell, they didn't find our feeds, so if they power their systems up again, we'll know about it."

"What did you learn before they shut it all down?" Mary asked.

"Somebody called 911; these people were sent out to seal the place off, keep local law enforcement out of there, like it was a top secret government site. There's something in that place that we missed — has to be, to justify that kind of security."

"Like what, Aaron?" I asked. "This isn't making sense. You're making it sound like Grissom's compound is a government installation."

"Yeah, that's what it looks like, all right. My gut says this is bigger than O'Hanlon's old drug ring. And don't forget, Lavrov seems to have been paying more attention to Jacksonville than to any of the other ports of entry along the East Coast."

"He put Grissom in there, right?" Mary asked. "To replace O'Hanlon's man?"

"Yeah. Joe Waters. Lavrov and his *Spetsnaz* buddy killed Waters and replaced him with Grissom. But Grissom's a known quantity; he worked for the guy running their operation in Savannah. He's got a long track record in southeast

Georgia; he's a local badass, not a superspy, if that's what you're thinking."

"Maybe they killed Waters because he stumbled over whatever they're hiding," I said. "They could have picked Grissom because they figured he was too far out of the loop to know any better."

"That's a possibility," Aaron said. "Mike and Bob will be here soon. They'll want to kick this around. I need to go collect my thoughts and check my traps before they get here. And there's one more thing before I forget."

"What's that?" I asked.

"There's no sign that they recognized you, Finn. We got that from listening in on Dixon and the others. Plus, Bobby said they thought you were just snooping for some local dealer. They didn't connect you to Mary, or what happened in Charleston."

"That may change," I said. "If they've got any pictures of me from either place, Lavrov might make the connection. He definitely knows Mary."

"Yeah, but they don't know who she's working for. And there won't be any images of you recovered from Grissom's compound. We took care of that. I need to go get to work."

"What about Jill?" Mary asked.

"She's still here. Once we finish up with Bob and Mike, she'll need to talk with both of you, time permitting."

"Sure," I said. "Thanks again, Aaron. And you, too, Mary. I appreciate your saving my sorry hide. I wouldn't have made a good handbag, anyway."

19

BOB AND MIKE JOINED MARY AND AARON AND ME JUST AS WE finished breakfast. Jill Hardwick came into the dining room shortly before Mike and Bob arrived. She sat apart from us, still eating.

"Just pretend I'm a fly on the wall," she said, after we all exchanged greetings with Mike and Bob. "I told the others that I just want to pick up as much background as I can."

"Good enough, Jill," Bob said. "Finn, it sounds like you kicked a hornets' nest the other night."

"Funny, but hornets' nest reminds me. I thought a wasp stung me right before I fell from that tree. That's what their tranquilizer dart felt like. Hit me on the side of the neck. Then I felt myself falling, and that was it. Out before I hit the ground, I guess."

"I remember the same feeling from when they got me in Charleston," Mary said.

"So you were up a tree, Finn?" Bob asked.

"Yes, to see over the wall. Sorry if I'm not making sense. I can't remember who knows what."

"That's all right," Mike said. "Glad you're okay, Finn. Any idea how they spotted you?"

"Yes, thanks to what Aaron told me a little while ago. He and Mary should tell the story, Mike. I don't remember much after the dart until they showed up and cut me loose. And what I do recall is scrambled."

"I know that feeling," Mary said. "It'll fall into place once you hear things from the beginning. It did for me, anyway."

"All right," Mike said. "Aaron and Mary, you're on. Finn?"

"Yes?"

"Chime in any time, if something comes to you."

"Okay."

"We first suspected Finn was in trouble about 24 hours ago," Aaron said. "Mary joined Jill and me for breakfast, and she was worried because she couldn't get in touch with Finn. Mary?"

"Finn called me the night before last, right before he left the motel to go to Grissom's place."

"Shit," I said.

"What's wrong?" Mary asked, as all eyes shifted to me.

"The motel. I forgot all about it. I left my duffle bag there."

"That's all taken care of," Aaron said. "We have it. Don't worry. Mary?"

"Finn told me he was going out on a night reconnaissance mission. He didn't say where. And we didn't discuss it beyond the fact that he was going. He didn't have much time to talk; he said he'd call me before breakfast the next morning. That would have been yesterday, about this time, when he was supposed to call. He didn't call me, so I tried to call him. I went straight to voicemail. So I told Aaron, and he took it from there. Aaron?"

"I put the team to work locating Finn's phone. In a few minutes, they called back. It was inside Grissom's perimeter, pretty much dead center in the compound. They gave me a position accurate within a meter, and Grissom's compound is about 100 meters square, so we figured Finn was in there. That wasn't part of the plan. He was supposed to check out their perimeter security and see if he spotted any activity that would show whether Grissom was there."

"Okay," Mike said. "Hold up for a bit. Finn, how long were you watching before they captured you? Tell us about your surveillance. Let's keep the chronology straight."

I nodded. "I got in position just after dark, night before last. There was a big live oak tree 25 yards outside the perimeter wall. Climbing up about 20 feet above ground gave me a good view of the back of the house and the pool area. I was there just long enough to get situated — say two or three minutes — when a woman came outside and started her yoga routine on the pool deck. There was a man with her, ogling her while she did her stretches. I was checking the wall and the ground inside for infrared beams when the dart hit me. I would guess I was only up the tree for about ten minutes."

"Any idea who the couple were?" Bob asked.

"Yes, but I only learned that later. Aaron should pick it back up to keep things in order."

"Right," Aaron said. "Mary and I figured Finn was definitely in trouble when we saw where his phone was. I made a few calls to set things in motion, and we got on the road about nine a.m. I coordinated the prep work over the phone while Mary drove.

"The team on the ground in Jacksonville stole a Humvee from a mid-level drug dealer; they put him out of commission so he couldn't get in the way after we took his vehicle. Our plan was to make it look like he was behind the attack. The team lined up weapons for us and watched Grissom's compound from a safe distance. There was no traffic in or out.

"We also used remote access to enable the microphone on Finn's phone so we could hear what was happening in its vicinity. From that, we picked up that they had Finn in what they referred to as the interrogation room. We later learned from listening to the two men watching over Finn that the 'interrogation room' was a soundproofed recording studio, but more on that later. Grissom was out of town and not expected back for several days.

"A man named Bert Dixon was in charge in Grissom's absence. Sylvia Smith was Dixon's live-in girlfriend. Dixon and Smith were the couple Finn saw out by the pool.

"Smith was one sadistic woman. Dixon and Grissom used her to interrogate people. Her interrogations were a regular entertainment feature. They even let the off-duty security men watch, sometimes. We got that from the videos we found."

"Excuse me, Aaron," Bob said, "but tell us about that security detail."

"Okay. This is out of chronological order. What we know about them, we learned when we attacked the compound."

"That's okay," Bob said. "What about them?"

"There were eight of them, all male. From their looks and their tattoos, they were ex-military, most likely booted out with dishonorable discharges. We questioned two of them briefly; those two had worked as mercenaries in the Middle East for a while.

"They didn't know much about the others, and we didn't press them on it. The other six were already dead, so it didn't matter much. We grilled them on who was in charge, and where they were holding Finn. That's how we learned about Dixon and Smith and the security control room. I'll tell you more about the control room in a bit, if that's all right. Back to Smith?"

"Sure. Thanks for letting me lead you off topic," Bob said.

"Not a problem," Aaron said. "Smith worked in one of Dixon's clubs. Her stage name was Sylvie Skins; she was a real vixen.

"There were two more men there who worked for Dixon — Bubba and Bobby were the only names we got for them. They were street muscle — didn't seem too bright. Dixon had them watching Finn.

"We got this from eavesdropping — not from the security detail — just so you know. Bobby was new in his job; it seemed like Bubba probably recruited him. Bobby was full of big talk about what he would make Sylvie do if he got a shot at her. Bubba tried to cool him off, convince him she was dangerous. Bobby wasn't listening. He had the hots for her, and she knew it. She made Bobby pay for that later.

"Dixon planned to wait until last night to let the drugs wear off before he put Sylvie to work questioning Finn. They had no clue who he was; there was no sign they connected him to Mary. They knew about Mary, but we'll get to that in a minute.

"Sylvie had brains, aside from being sadistic and an exhibitionist. She and Dixon seemed more like partners than girlfriend and boss. They had two telephone conversations with somebody we think was Grissom, but we only heard their end of the calls.

"Both calls were about tracking down the woman responsible for the Charleston 'problem,' because the boss wanted her brought to the Exumas. Dixon said he had people working on it. They questioned 'the shrink.' That would be Samantha Peterson. She gave them Mary's address, but Mary vanished after his two guys got busted for breaking in her place after they questioned her shrink. Everybody still with me?" Aaron asked, making eye contact with each member of his audience.

Satisfied that we were following his story, Aaron said, "Okay, that's about it for the background. Let's move on to the rescue. By the time Mary and I picked up the Humvee and the weapons from our support team, we knew what we wanted to do. Mary, speak up if I miss something, okay?"

"I will, but so far, I can't add a thing."

Aaron nodded. "Thanks. There was no good way for us to sneak into the compound. All their security was geared to prevent that, so we opted to do what they weren't prepared for — a full-on frontal assault.

"We waited until Dixon and Smith were in the interrogation room with Finn. Bobby and Bubba were in there, too. We were keeping track of them using Finn's phone. Bubba had it in his pocket most of the time. We overheard him earlier, telling Bobby that the interrogation room was soundproof, so that's why we waited until they were in there to mount our assault. Sylvie was planning to make an example of Bobby to scare Finn into cooperating, so we knew there wasn't a huge rush.

"Once we made our move, I used an M72 to breach the gate, and Mary drove the Humvee through what was left. I blew the front door of the house off its hinges with 12-gauge rifled slugs, and we eliminated the security team in the confusion. We questioned the last two after we disabled them, and they told us the rest of what we needed to know, including how to get into the security control room.

"The security control room was equipped with monitors for all their surveillance systems. That includes the perimeter security system. I'll come back to that in a minute. It also was set up as a recording studio with gear to capture audio and video feeds from the interrogation room, which I mentioned was sound-proof. That meant Dixon and the others didn't hear our assault.

"Mary and I sat in the control room and watched Smith — Sylvie Skins — tormenting Bobby. Supposedly, that was to scare Finn, but it was clear that she mostly did it to amuse herself and Dixon. And because Bobby pissed her off, what with his lusting after her.

"When she finally turned her attention to Finn, Mary and I made our move. We went into the studio and killed Sylvie and Bubba. We kneecapped Dixon and grilled him before we finished him off. Bobby was a bloody mess by then, hog-tied and gagged. Old Sylvie did a number on him. We removed his gag and let him tell us what he knew, which wasn't much. Then we put him out of his misery.

"I stayed behind to do a little stage management while Mary got Finn out of there. Once I set the scene to look like a rival gang wiped out the crew at Grissom's place, I called the support team for a pickup.

"We left the Humvee to point the authorities to the local rivals, and we cleared out. Any questions so far?"

"Did you learn anything about Grissom that we didn't already know?" Mike asked.

"A bit," Aaron said. "He's at a meeting in the Bahamas, down in the Exumas. We think Lavrov's having a conference. Several of his direct reports are there. Our best guess is Grissom's peers from Savannah, Charleston, and Miami are part of it. We're working to pin down exactly where they are."

"Does that mean Lavrov's letting them see his face, finally?" Bob asked.

"Maybe," Aaron said. "We have no way of knowing. I suppose he could be in disguise. Or maybe he's got somebody else running the meeting. He may be there, but staying out of sight. Or maybe he's not even there."

"Right," Bob said. "Sorry for the interruption. Please go ahead."

Aaron nodded. "We picked up some other interesting facts, too. You asked how they spotted Finn. They have a prototype installation of the latest thermal imaging hardware — the stuff that's still in development for the Defense Department. No old-fashioned active infrared stuff for them. And it's amazing. It's no wonder they spotted Finn."

"That equipment's all classified, isn't it?" Bob asked.

"That's right," Aaron said.

"How could they have gotten their hands on it?" Mike asked.

"Good question. But it gets better. We were no sooner out of there than a federal special ops team sealed off the area."

"A federal special ops team?" Mike said. "Are you sure about that? I would have figured a neighbor might have called 911 after you blew the gate. Could it have been a high-end SWAT team? Maybe local law enforcement was already watching the place, or something."

"Come on Mike. I know the difference between a SWAT team and what we saw. This unit was platoon-sized, maybe 100 troops. And besides, they were setting up a perimeter to keep people out; they weren't trying to catch whoever was inside. It was almost like they knew Dixon and company were toast and didn't care. They were worried about a follow-up assault. The big question is what they were defending."

"Are you saying they were *protecting* something at Grissom's place?" Mike asked.

"Exactly," Aaron said.

"And how do you know they were feds?"

"We were monitoring the communications for state and local law enforcement. They were all wondering what the feds were up to."

"Why would the feds be sealing off Grissom's place?" Mike asked. "Did they even attempt to rescue the people inside?"

"No. We were tapped into all the systems in the compound, and we broke the encryption on the feds' comm network a little while after they got set up. They knew everybody in there was dead. They were focused on keeping people out of there first, and finding out who hit the place, second."

"Are we clean?" Mike asked.

"Sparkling clean," Aaron said.

"You sure the surveillance system at Grissom's didn't record any of you during the rescue?"

"We wiped all of that; that was one reason we tapped the system before we left. We left no video or audio recordings that have a trace of us."

"That will make somebody suspicious," Bob said. "It won't take much for them to spot gaps in the surveillance."

"You're right, but by the time they figure it out, they will have wasted a lot of time, and they still won't know who pulled off the raid, or why. The only thing we couldn't clean up was what Dixon and Smith told the person they were talking to on the phone — Grissom, most likely. He knows they captured someone who was watching the compound, but like I said, they don't have a clue about who Finn is, or who he's working for."

"Good job," Mike said. "Thanks, everybody. Take a breather; Bob and I will be in my cabin for a while. We need to kick this around with a few others. Let's regroup here at 1500."

After Mike and Bob left, Mary and I went back to our cabin and crashed, setting an alarm for two-thirty.

20

AT THREE O'CLOCK, MARY AND I FOUND AARON SITTING IN THE dining area of the main building with Bob and Mike.

"Sorry to keep you waiting," I said.

"No, you didn't," Mike said. "Bob and I just sat down. Before you get comfortable, though, Jill wants to spend a little time with you, Mary. She's waiting in her cabin."

Mary frowned. "I'm okay, really."

"We think you are," Bob said. "But humor us, please. She won't keep you for long. Mike and I have some admin stuff we want to cover with these two, anyway. If you miss anything, Finn can fill you in."

"All right, if you say so. Finn?"

"Yes?"

"Pay attention; there will be a quiz later."

"Yes, ma'am."

When she was gone, Bob asked, "How is she holding up, Finn?"

"We were too tired to do anything but nap just now. But she's as good as new, the best I can tell."

"Aaron, how did she deal with the attack?" Mike asked. "You felt okay about working with her?"

"Yes, there were no problems there. But I have to say, I never worked with anybody like her before."

"Tell us more," Bob said.

"Well, most of my field-ops time was spent with military people. She's different."

"Different how?" Mike asked.

"Stone cold," Aaron said. "And she's a loner. It was like watching a shark feeding, or a snake, or something. She's like a machine once the action starts. No nerves, no emotion. No wasted motion. I blew the door down, and she went in first. After that, all I did was follow her and stay out of her way.

"The first two guys came running around a corner at us with semi-automatic, sawed-off shotguns. The next thing I knew, they were sprawled on the floor. I never even saw her move, it happened so fast. Two rounds, two bodies. I don't even think she blinked. She just kept moving, never broke her stride. I felt like excess baggage, like I didn't even need to be there."

"You probably didn't," I said. "She's accustomed to working alone, remember?"

"Yeah. I noticed. She never even looked back at me. She picked up one of their shotguns on her way by and moved to the corner they came from. Dropped to the floor and stuck the shotgun around the corner with her left hand and cut loose. Emptied the magazine.

"Then she rolled around the corner and finished off the four that were writhing on the floor there. Man, that buckshot made a mess. Four more rounds from her pistol, but that was mercy killing. They were going to die anyway.

"I was worried that she would kill them all before we got to question any of them. But the next one stepped out of a door on the right side of the hallway with his hands up. He said, 'Don't shoot me — I'll help you with whatever you want.' She shot him in both shoulders, and he fell.

"When he fell, we saw his buddy behind him, pistol at the ready, planning to drop us, I guess. They probably figured we'd be distracted by the one who tried to surrender. The second one dropped his pistol and raised his hands. Mary put one in his thigh; it knocked him down. Shattered his femur.

"Then she spoke for the first time. She said, 'Cover me,' and dove through the door the last two had come from. She came out in a few seconds and said, 'That's it. Found their duty roster. Everybody's accounted for. Let's see what these two know.' And we've told you the rest."

"That's Mary," I said. "Nine rounds, eight men down. She was pissed about that extra round, I'll bet."

"She didn't seem pissed, but she did feel the need to explain it to me. Said she figured the one with his hands up was a decoy, and she didn't want him to be able to shoot when the other one showed up. Since he wasn't holding a weapon, she didn't know which hand he would use, so she disabled both."

"Who questioned those two? You? Or Mary?" Mike asked.

"Both of us. But she was the one holding the knife. And she finished them off when we were done."

"Two more rounds?" I asked.

"No. She used the knife."

"And when you two crashed into the studio," Mike asked, "who did the shooting?"

"Mary. Like I said, she's fast. She questioned Dixon, too. And then killed him."

"It sounds like she's functioning all right," Mike said. "How was she afterward, Finn?"

"Fine. Like she used to be."

"Great. Jill's feeling good about her, but she wanted the chance to see how Mary reacted to this operation before she gave us the all-clear."

Mike's cellphone rang.

"Yes?" he answered.

He listened for a moment and said, "Good. Thanks. Come on over, both of you."

Disconnecting the call, he put the phone away. "Perfect timing. That was Jill. Mary's back in the game. Let's grab some coffee or juice while we're waiting for them."

"Aaron got an intelligence update this morning after we broke up," Mike said, once Mary and Jill joined us. "What's new, Aaron?"

"The federal special ops people disappeared about daylight — no sign they were ever there. The local police are crawling all over Grissom's place now, investigating the 'massacre,' as they're calling it. The feds told the locals they were reacting to a report of terrorist activity involving a nuclear threat. It turned out to be bogus, they said."

"That sounds like bullshit, to me," I said. "What do you suppose they were really doing?"

"We don't know yet, but we're working on it. There must have been something there that they didn't want the locals or anybody else to know about, but nobody's figured out what it was, yet. Or maybe they were worried that there might have been something, and then they learned that it wasn't there."

"So the feds went in and cleared whatever it was?" Mike asked.

"That was our first assumption, but it's not consistent with the facts that are emerging. We're monitoring what the people on site are reporting. So far, they haven't found anything we didn't already know about from when Mary and I were there. The structure is intact; they didn't break through any walls or floors looking for hiding places. There's nothing obviously missing — no voids where there used to be furniture."

"How can the police tell about the furniture?" Bob asked.

"There's enough recorded video in the surveillance control room for them to see that nothing's missing."

"Does the video show what the feds were up to?" Mike asked. "I thought you said your people were monitoring those feeds."

"Yes," Aaron said. "They've been watching ever since Mary and I left there. Here's the really odd thing: the feds never set foot in the compound. They just threw up the perimeter, and after a couple of hours, they cleared out."

"This isn't making any sense," Mike said.

"Right," Aaron said. "It sure isn't. We're missing something. The feds didn't want anybody in there, but they didn't go in, either."

"Could they have been reacting to a false alarm?" Bob asked. "You said earlier your people tapped their encrypted comm links, didn't you?"

"Yes, we were listening to their comms," Aaron said. "All we got was tactical stuff related to establishing and maintaining the perimeter. The only time we heard anything different was right before they pulled out. The unit commander told his subordinates they had the all clear from up the line, and they should clear the area ASAP."

"Your people are still monitoring the situation, I take it?" Mike asked.

"Yes. The police are going over the place with a fine-tooth

comb. They tried to get warrants to search the compound several times over the last couple of years, for various reasons. They never managed to get one approved. Now that they have a crime scene to justify their search, they're being extra thorough. They're taking their time. If they find anything, we'll know about it. But for now, that's all I have on the compound."

"Okay," Mike said. "Anything else?"

"Yes," Aaron said. "About the meeting in the Exumas ... "

"Tell us," Bob said.

"We hacked the Bahamian Customs database. Grissom's private plane flew into Exuma International Airport; that's where they cleared into the country."

"The Exumas stretch south maybe 150 miles from Nassau," I said. "There are over 350 islands in the Exumas. Is that the airport that serves George Town?"

"Yes," Aaron said.

"So he landed at the south end of the Exumas, but there are still a lot of islands not far from there. Any clue as to where he went?"

"No, not yet. He and the pilot gave Customs a resort in George Town as their local address. The others flew in there, too. But there's no meeting going on at the resort. The pilots are hanging out there, but Grissom and his pals are somewhere else."

"How about the pilot? Or pilots?" Mary asked. "You said they're still at the resort."

"Yes, so far," Aaron said.

"So we could snatch one of them and question him," Mary said.

"Probably so," I said, "but the odds are good that they don't know where the meeting's being held. If you snatch one of them, it's just going to alert Grissom and his buddies."

"Finn's right," Aaron said, "but we're working another angle. Remember when you and I heard Dixon and his girlfriend talking to someone on the phone after they caught Finn?"

"Yes. About how I disappeared after Dixon's boys got arrested for breaking into my townhouse," Mary said.

"Right. And about the guy they caught looking over the wall. We've got all the cellphone numbers for all the people who were in the compound. We're combing through them; we probably even have Grissom's number. Once we make sense of that data, we'll look for that call we overheard. Given that we know about the timing, and that it was to or from Dixon's phone, we should be able to pin down where Grissom's phone was."

"How long is that going to take?" Mike asked.

"I don't have a good estimate," Aaron said. "It's going to take a lot of guesswork, then some trial and error, unfortunately."

"We need to get our hands on Grissom — alive, and able to answer questions," Mike said. "And as soon as we can. He's the key to finding out what's in that compound, what the special ops team was defending."

"Maybe," Bob said. "Or maybe not. But he's our best option right now. Think you can snatch him out of the meeting, Finn? Mary?"

"Well, we can handle interrogating him," I said, "but we may not want to snatch him. Too much chance he would be missed before we can act on what we learn from him."

"I agree," Mary said. "Depending on where they're having the meeting, it might be better to interrogate him there."

"But what about the other attendees?" Bob asked. "There's still the risk that they'll discover what's happening."

"Not if they're dead," Mary said. "They were on our list of targets a few weeks ago, weren't they?"

"You're proposing to go in and wipe them all out but Grissom, then?" Mike asked.

"We could spare one or two, in case we want to question somebody else," I said. "That way, we might be able to verify what we get from Grissom."

"What about logistics?" Bob asked. "You said there were 350 islands in the Exumas, Finn. I'm guessing a lot of them are uninhabited, or private. Correct?"

"Yes. There are plenty of both kinds. We'll need a boat. Ideally, something that will blend in. That's an area where there are a lot of sailboats with couples aboard, but *Island Girl* is too far away to be practical. We might be able to charter something in Nassau."

"Or Miami, for sure," Mary said. "That would add maybe 24 to 36 hours to our travel time, though."

"Besides," I said, "if we sail in from the States, we'll have to clear customs going into the Bahamas and again when we return to the States. Even with false identities, that's a paper trail. Nassau would be better."

"I can solve that problem," Mike said.

We all turned to look at him. He grinned. "I left my boat at Paradise Island, in Nassau. She's been there a couple of months, now."

"What kind of boat?" I asked. "I didn't know you had a boat."

"A Bermuda 40," Mike said. "I've had her for 30 years."

"I didn't even know you sailed," I said.

"I don't get in as much sailing as I'd like to, but whenever I can get down there, I take her out."

"How much water does she draw with the board up?" I asked.

"A few inches over four feet," Mike said.

"Perfect for where we're headed," I said, "and that solves the customs clearance problems. We'll just fly in, sail her down to wherever, do our job, and put her back in Nassau."

"We'll book the two of you into a villa in Nassau under whatever names you're using," Aaron said. "And we'll make sure it looks occupied the whole time, so you'll have an alibi, should the need arise."

"We won't need an alibi," Mary said.

"Not one to share with the authorities," Aaron said. "But one for misdirection in case anybody starts digging into airline reservations, or the customs and immigration databases."

"How long will it take you to get from Nassau to George Town?" Bob asked.

"It's daytime sailing," Mike said. "You have to eyeball the water depth; there are lots of coral heads between Nassau and the northern end of the Exumas. And even along the west side of the island chain. Maybe two or three days. But I thought they were going to be there until next week, didn't you say?"

"Yes," Aaron said. "That's what we picked up. That's cutting it a little fine."

"There's a faster route," I said.

"How's that?" Mike asked.

"Southeast from New Providence Island until we're south of the Yellow Bank, then up to Ship Channel Cay. That's a little over 30 miles — easy to do while we have good light for dodging the coral heads. From there, we'll head out into Exuma Sound, and we'll have deep water all the way to George Town. It's 100 miles from Ship Channel Cay to George Town, so we'll enter the harbor in daylight the morning after we leave Nassau."

"Sounds good," Mike said. "Let's get you on your way. By the time you're out in Exuma Sound, Aaron should know more about where the meeting is. You okay with that, Aaron?"

"Sure. Let me make a call; I'll line up a charter to fly you into Nassau tonight and get you fixed up with a villa as close to Mike's boat as we can manage."

"Mary?" Bob asked.

"Yes?"

"You up for this?"

"Yes."

"Finn?"

"Yes. I've always wanted to sail a Bermuda 40."

"Why haven't you bought one, then?" Mike asked. "There are plenty on the market these days."

"They're beautiful. That's why," I said.

Mike frowned. "Yes. So?"

"So I need something nondescript. Yours will be fine for where we're going. There are always lots of rich Americans on fancy boats in the Bahamas. But down where I hang out most of the time, a Bermuda 40 would attract too much attention."

"Let's do it, then," Mike said. "Have fun, but be careful with my boat."

"We will," Mary said. "Come on, sailor. Let's pack our bags."

"Yes, ma'am. We're outta here."

21

Mary and I slept in and ate a late breakfast at a restaurant in the mega-yacht marina at Paradise Island. We weren't in a big hurry to get away; the coral heads in the shallows would be easier to see if we waited until the sun was high in the sky.

"Man, this place is a serious tourist trap," Mary said, as she gazed at the people wandering around the marina and the adjacent hotel grounds.

"Yes," I said. "It used to be called Hog Island. There was a seedy hotel on the beach, and a few cheap local restaurants. Other than that, it was all scrub palmetto."

"How long ago was that?"

I shrugged. "Thirty years, give or take. Before my time, but when I first came here, this resort was only partly built. The locals were unhappy about the changes; they would tell you all about it. One old guy had pictures. The old places were dying off by then, but it was nothing like it is now."

"There are some incredible boats in here," Mary said. "I don't see anything that looks like a boat we might sail."

"No. Mike's boat's not in here. There's another marina for the people like us. It's been here a long time; it's at the foot of the bridge that goes to New Providence Island."

"New Providence Island?"

"That's where Nassau is," I said.

"But I thought we were in Nassau."

"Maybe. I don't know where the city limits are — never worried about it. It's not a long walk across the bridge, anyway. And then you're in Nassau for sure. You about ready to go check out Mike's boat?"

"Sure. I wonder why he named her *Isabella*. Think that's his wife's name?" Mary asked, drinking the last of her coffee.

"I don't know. You'd have to ask him."

"I thought you knew him pretty well, from the Army."

I laughed.

"What's funny?" she asked.

"Nothing, really. Just the notion of my knowing him from the Army. I only knew him by reputation. There was a wide gulf between a brand new Second Lieutenant like me and a Lieutenant General like Mike."

"Oh," she said. "It just seems like you four are cut from the same cloth, you and Aaron and Mike and my uncle."

"There's a lot of shared experience, I guess. Aaron and I were buddies; we were the same rank. We served under your Uncle Bob, so we knew him, but only to work for him. We sure didn't socialize with Bob. And Mike was senior to Bob."

"But we're all on a first name basis, now," Mary said.

"Yes, and you have no idea how strange that feels to me and Aaron. Anyway, I have no clue why Mike's boat is named *Isabella*. You ready to go?"

"Yes."

I left enough cash on the table to cover our breakfast and

got to my feet. Mary stood up and swung her backpack over her shoulder. Hefting my own pack, I followed her out of the restaurant. We left most of our luggage in the villa Aaron rented for us.

He sent a couple to take our place there. In case anybody tracked us from Florida to Nassau, it would appear that we spent our entire time lazing around, like wannabe rich people.

Once out of the resort's grounds, I led the way to the small marina where *Isabella* was waiting for us. We spotted her at once. Her shiny, flag-blue hull and gleaming varnish made her look like a piece of jewelry nestled between the larger vessels berthed on either side of her.

"Wow," Mary said, pausing as we walked onto the dock where *Isabella* was tied. "She looks like a showpiece. But she's not as big as *Island Girl*. I thought she would be 40 feet, because you and Mike called her a Bermuda 40."

"She is," I said.

"But *Island Girl's* only 34 feet."

"*Island Girl's* a workhorse," I said. "*Isabella's* a thoroughbred. She's not as beefy as *Island Girl*, not as broad in the beam. And she sits a lot lower in the water."

"Is she as seaworthy?" Mary asked, worry lines on her forehead as she studied *Isabella*.

"Yes, definitely. The Bermuda 40s have been around a long time. They've won more than their share of ocean races, some under wild conditions. She's a go-anywhere boat. And she'll be faster than *Island Girl*."

"If you say so. She sure is pretty."

I stepped over the lifelines onto *Isabella's* side deck and turned to give Mary a hand aboard. We went back to the cockpit, and I dialed the combination Mike gave me into the lock on the companionway hatch. Below deck, we stashed our backpacks in the first empty lockers we found.

Mary spent a few minutes exploring the narrow space below deck while I looked at the instruments in the panel over the chart table. When she finished poking around, she joined me, and I talked her through what I found.

"Questions?" I asked.

She shook her head. "Not about the electronics. That all looks straightforward. But we need groceries. The cupboard's bare."

"Okay. Let's lock her up and walk across the bridge. We should be able to find the basics pretty quickly."

"If you're in a hurry, I guess we could stock up down the way somewhere," Mary said.

"This isn't like the Eastern Caribbean. There's not really anywhere to stock up until we get to George Town, and there's not much there. Groceries are hard to find in the Exumas. Nassau's our best bet."

"Lead on, then, skipper."

We spent an hour buying staples and enough canned goods to keep us going for two weeks. When we got back aboard *Isabella,* it was time to go. I unlocked the companionway again, and we took the bags of food below.

"Give me a hand getting her out of the slip," I said, as Mary started opening the lockers in the galley. "There'll be time to stow everything while we motor through the harbor."

"All right, sailor. You get the engine running, and I'll be right up. I need to use the head, first. Too much coffee."

A few minutes later, I was working my way through the traffic, headed east through the harbor. Mary finished putting our groceries away and came up to join me in the cockpit.

"Busy place," she said. "Did you want to plug a course into the chart plotter? I can take the helm while you do that."

"Not yet; there's no need. It will be eyeball navigation until we get to the cut."

"Which cut?"

"Ship Channel Cut. It's 30-odd miles east. It'll take us out into Exuma Sound; then we can relax."

"Want some sail up?" she asked.

"Not just yet. See that beacon sticking up out there off our port bow?"

Mary shaded her eyes with her hand. "Got it. What about it?"

"That marks Porgee Rocks. Once we pass it, I'll put more south in our course. We'll see what the wind's doing then. We might get to sail if we're lucky. We'll hold a southeasterly course and dodge the coral heads on the Yellow Bank. Once we're past the worst of them, we'll head northeast until we pick up the beacon just north of Ship Channel Cay, and we'll steer on it. We've got maybe five or six hours before we get there, depending on the wind and the current."

"You think we'll have to motor the whole way? That stinks."

"I agree, but the wind's fluky through here, and we need to make it through the cut while we have daylight. Once we're out in Exuma Sound, we can probably have a nice sail all the way to George Town. And there won't be much traffic out there."

"No?"

"No. Most people head south down the west side of the Exumas. It's daylight sailing. You have to watch for shallow spots, but the ride is smooth, because the islands block the wind chop we'll find out in the Sound."

"It looks like we'll have a nice, clear night for it," Mary said. "I hope there's a good breeze."

"There should be; we won't have much land to the east of us, so we should have good wind."

"Sounds nice, sailor. Clear night, nice breeze, and no company except each other. I've missed that."

"Me, too."

"This water's beautiful, Finn." She raised herself enough to get a look at the depth sounder. "But it's really shallow. I see what you mean about eyeball navigation."

"The color of the water gives you a good idea of the depth if you know the kind of bottom under it," I said. "It's mostly sand, and the lighter the water's color, the shallower it is. We want to stay in the turquoise to blue water. If it looks white, it's shallow. The darker the blue, the deeper it is."

"Okay. But can't you just plot a course to pass the shallow stuff and the coral heads?"

"In theory yes. There are two problems with that, though. The sandy bottom changes often; the shoals move with the currents. A good squall with a lot of wind and wave action can wreak havoc with charted depths. And the locations of the coral heads aren't charted with much accuracy. See that big dark mass in the turquoise water about 75 yards off the starboard bow?"

"Yes. Is that a deep hole, or something? Darker's deeper, right?"

"Right, except that's a big coral head. Notice how sharply defined the edge of the dark area is?"

"Yes, and it looks dark brown, almost black, now that we're closer to it."

"Good observation. If that were a deeper spot, the color would change from lighter to darker blue, but the transition would be more gradual. With a little practice, you can learn to estimate depth within a foot or so, if you know the color of the bottom in the area you're crossing."

"This is nerve-wracking, Finn." Mary was watching the coral head as we passed it a few yards off our starboard beam. "That would tear the bottom out of a boat if you hit it at any speed. And is that another one, straight ahead?"

"No. That's the shadow of that cloud that's just a little ahead of us."

"How can you tell?"

"I've been watching it. Its shape and position are changing as the cloud moves."

"Like I said, nerve-wracking."

"You get used to it. It's not that tough, but you do have to pay attention. It's not like sailing in open water, that's for sure."

"I'll let you steer, if that's okay. I'll take my turn once we're in the Sound."

"That's fine," I said. "But let me know if you change your mind."

"Maybe. But for now, I'll keep watching the bottom and the depth until it all makes sense. You want lunch?"

"Sure, if you're ready."

"I'll make conch salad sandwiches. I'm worried that stuff won't keep."

"It should be okay for a few days in the fridge," I said. "You watched that woman making it; it's fresh."

"I know. That's what she said, but I'm eager to taste it."

"Then go for it."

"One sandwich? Or two?"

"Two, please," I said, as she ducked through the companionway and went below.

22

"HOW ARE YOU HOLDING UP?" I ASKED MARY. SHE TOOK THE helm right after we entered Exuma Sound.

"I'm okay; I've only been steering for three hours. You don't want a nap?"

"You know how it is; I'm too keyed up to sleep right now."

We were on a southeasterly course, making close to seven knots under sail alone. If the northeast wind held through the night, we would be anchored in George Town's Elizabeth Harbour sometime between eight and nine o'clock tomorrow morning.

About ten or twelve miles east of the Exumas, we were having a glorious sail. There was an easterly swell running, and the wind was just behind our beam, holding us nice and steady as we rode the swell. When we crested a wave, we could pick up an occasional flash from the two-second-red-flashing beacon on Highbourne Cay. Otherwise, there was nothing to remind us that there were other people anywhere near us.

"I'm surprised we haven't heard from Aaron," Mary said.

"Cellphone service in the Bahamas is spotty unless you're

close to an area with enough people to justify a cell tower. Even then, it's not a sure bet. I should dig out the satellite phone and call him."

"Bring it up here so we can both hear what he has to say, okay?"

"Yes," I said, as I went down the companionway ladder. "Not sure it would get a signal below deck, anyway."

In two minutes, I was back in the cockpit. Mary snuggled against me as we watched the screen on my Phorcys-provided, encrypted satellite phone. Once it acquired a signal, I called Aaron.

"Finn?"

"You got both of us, Aaron," I said.

"Good. I've been trying to reach you for the last couple of hours."

"Yeah," I said. "Sorry about that. I've been in the States too long. I forgot how flaky cellphones can be in the Bahamas. They show they have service on the screen, but ... "

"Right. Where are you, now?"

"About twelve or fifteen miles southeast of Highbourne Cay, out in Exuma Sound. We're having a grand sail; Mike's boat is really sweet."

"I'll tell him when I talk to him in the morning. Meanwhile, we may have something on Grissom's location."

"You sound like you're hedging."

"You're right. Bahamian cellphone service, again. He was connected to a cell site in George Town when he talked with Dixon the other day, but that's all we got. The service provider down there strips the location data to save bandwidth, or some such bullshit."

"So we're supposed to go to George Town and look under every rock, huh?"

"Something like that. We'll narrow the scope for you. We have the position of the tower that supported his call. We've put it at the center of a circle on a surveillance photo we hacked from the DEA. It's tedious work, but the folks are picking locations in the circle that look like they could host a small, private meeting. Then they dig up whatever's available on the possible sites. Once they finish their research, you should be able to just knock on a few doors and ask for him. When somebody shoots at you, you'll know you found the right place."

"You do good work, Aaron," Mary said.

"We try. That's all I have for you on Grissom so far. Glad you're having a nice sail. Wish I were with you guys."

"One of these days, you'll have to join us on *Island Girl*," I said. "See how the other half lives. Anything else going on up your way?"

"Yes, but we haven't figured out what. Turns out there's a modular data center tucked away in an outbuilding in Grissom's compound. The police didn't figure that out right away. The building looks like something to house landscaping equipment. It's screened from the main house by tall shrubbery — barely noticeable. It was locked from the outside, so the police knew nobody was in there. Or if they were locked inside, they weren't going anywhere. So they saved it for last.

"The building's not that big; maybe the size of a triple garage. But when they got around to breaking in and checking it out, they didn't find much. Nothing but a lawn tractor and garden tools, until one of their people noticed the interior was smaller than the exterior. There was a false wall in the back that cut off eight feet in one dimension and the width of the building — maybe 30 feet — in the other. The only way into the hidden space was through the attic. You with me so far?"

"Yes," I said. "There was a data center in there? But what about power, and cooling and everything?"

"It turns out you can buy an eight-foot by twenty-foot standard shipping container all tricked out with everything you need for your own server farm. They even come with backup power and air-conditioning."

"That doesn't sound very big," I said. "How much of a data center could that be?"

"A powerful one, given how small all that stuff is nowadays. A thousand servers, give or take a few."

"What were they doing with it? Keeping their books? Storing all their files?" Mary asked.

"We can't tell. It was scrubbed clean. The servers were 'acid-washed,' as the geeks say. There's no data left."

"So that's what the feds were doing," I said. "Making sure nobody found it before everything was erased."

"You win the prize," Aaron said.

"But you said the feds never set foot in the compound," I said.

"That's right. And we didn't leave anybody alive in there. I checked the whole area inside the wall. Even checked the padlock on that outbuilding."

"So was there evidence that somebody went inside the locked building?" Mary asked. "While the feds were there, I mean?"

"No. Our bunch says the data was probably erased remotely. The feds just needed to make sure nobody got in there and shut things down before the servers were wiped."

"So now we have more questions for our friend Grissom," I said.

"You got it."

"Can you tell anything about data traffic in and out of the server farm?" Mary asked.

"Good for you, Mary," Aaron said. "Now that we know about it, we're trying to get some idea of the volume and the sources. The actual data in and out was no doubt encrypted, but we may learn something about who was communicating with the servers."

"What could they have been doing?" I asked.

"I told you, Finn. We don't know."

"Yes, I understood that. I meant to ask if you could come up with a list of uses for that kind of computer power."

"Well, yes," Aaron said, "but it could be almost anything. Record keeping, as Mary said, or hosting bots to manipulate social media. It could even be used for hacking into other people's databases. There's no end of mischief that you could get into with that much horsepower. That's why we need Grissom alive."

"Once we find him, we'll keep that in mind," I said. "Anything else?"

"No, not now. When do you think you'll get to George Town?"

"We should be in the harbor with the anchor set by nine o'clock."

"Okay. Call me before you anchor. Maybe we'll have more on Grissom's location by then. My guess is he won't be in George Town itself. Probably at a private island hideaway."

"There are a lot of those down there," I said.

"I'm getting that impression. Have a good sail, and we'll talk in the morning." With that, he disconnected the call.

"A server farm," Mary said. "I wouldn't have pictured something called a server farm fitting in a shipping container. I thought it would be in a raised floor computer room, like the main data center on the University campus."

"You're ahead of me. I don't know enough about it to even form an image. I've heard the term, and I know it has something to do with computer networks, but that's about it."

"Why would a drug lord have his own data center?" Mary asked. "It's not making sense to me. Grissom took over from a guy named Joe Waters, remember? Lavrov put him in there after he got rid of Waters."

"Right. Where are you going with this, Mary?"

"Back to Dailey and O'Hanlon."

When I met Mary a few months ago, she was on the run from a man named Rory O'Hanlon. O'Hanlon was the most powerful and best-connected criminal in the U.S. Francis X. Dailey, a big-time developer, kept O'Hanlon's books and laundered the profits from his drug empire. O'Hanlon discovered Dailey was skimming. He hired Mary to kill Dailey and recover the stolen money and the records he kept.

Mary was on her way to turn over everything to O'Hanlon when he sent his people to kill her and recover his property. She knew too much for him to let her live. Mary didn't react well to being double-crossed, and that cost O'Hanlon his life.

The records Mary recovered listed payoffs to corrupt government officials, many at the highest levels. To avoid exposure, those officials wanted Mary eliminated. Just as chaos began to develop, the Russian, Uri Lavrov, started rebuilding O'Hanlon's operation. By then, Mary and I were working for Phorcys.

"What about Dailey and O'Hanlon?" I asked.

"They built this whole operation, remember? This huge, corrupt empire."

"Yes. So what's your point?"

"I stole all their records from a safe in Dailey's bedroom; they were all on one thumb drive. Their books, who they were paying off, everything. They didn't have a data center. They didn't need one."

"By damn, you're right. So whose data center is that? And why were the feds so eager to make sure nobody got the files from those servers?"

"Exactly my questions, sailor. Should we call Aaron back? Share that with him?"

"Right now, he's focused on tactical problems, like where Grissom is, and the sources and destinations of the traffic on those servers. That's how we'll find out who was using them and what for. Another phone call will just slow him down."

"If you say so, Finn."

"We'll mention it to him in the morning. Those questions won't change anything tonight."

"Okay," she said.

I slid into the narrow space behind the helm, my hip against hers. I nudged her with my elbow and put my hands on the rim of the helm.

"And speaking of tonight, you should go below and try to get some sleep. We need to hit the ground running tomorrow."

"Aye, aye, skipper. See you in four hours."

She gave me a kiss, then went down the companionway ladder and disappeared into the shadows of the main cabin.

23

THE REPETITIVE FLASHES OF LIGHT ACROSS MY EYELIDS WOKE ME up. Disoriented, I opened one eye just enough to get a look at my surroundings. On a boat — that much I could tell. The flash was sunlight coming through the porthole on the opposite side of the cabin.

I was stretched out on a settee, lying on my right side with my head toward the bow. As the boat rolled, the sunlight swept over my face.

Then I focused on the sounds: the swish of the hull slicing through the water, the sighing of the wind in the rigging, and a recurring gurgle. A puff of wind through the companionway brought the smell of fresh-brewed coffee. That explained the gurgle — a percolator.

I sat up and shook my head, rubbing my eyes and looking around. This was Mike Killington's boat, *Isabella*, I remembered. And Mary was with me. She must be on watch. But she should have awakened me an hour or two before sunup.

Standing up and grasping the overhead handrail, I shuffled back to the galley. The color of the coffee bubbling through the glass knob on top of the percolator told me it was ready. I switched off the gas and turned to take a step up the companionway ladder. Peering out, I saw Mary sprawled behind the helm. Her head was tipped back, her gaze on a pair of frigate birds gliding along in our wind wake.

"Good morning," I said.

"Hey, sleepy-head," she said, looking down at me and grinning.

"You were supposed to wake me after your four-hour watch."

"I know. But I decided to let you sleep. I was doing okay, and you weren't recovered from the stress that vixen put you through."

"Which vixen?"

"Dixon's stripper girlfriend."

"Oh, *that* vixen."

"What vixen did you think I meant?"

"I'll take the fifth on that one."

"Pour us some coffee and get up here before you get yourself in more trouble than you can handle. I'll show you which *vixen* you should worry about."

"Yes, ma'am. Err, I mean no, ma'am."

"Shut up and get the coffee. I'm glad you're feeling well enough to be a smart-ass."

I filled two mugs and set them on the bridge deck right outside the companionway. After pouring the rest of the coffee into a thermos, I climbed into the cockpit and handed Mary a mug. I stashed the thermos in a corner of the cockpit's footwell and picked up my mug, joining Mary on the narrow seat behind the helm.

"Thanks for letting me sleep," I said. "I guess I needed it."

"I would say so. I checked on you a few times to make sure

you weren't going to roll off the settee. You were out cold. One time I tried to push you back from the edge, but it was like shoving a bag of wet sand. You didn't roll out of the berth, anyway. It was a calm night."

"I didn't think to rig a lee cloth before I crashed. Too worn out, I guess. But I'm surprised you didn't do it earlier, when you took your nap."

"I slept up in the forward berth — didn't need a lee cloth to hold me in. The ventilation is better up there and it was still hot when I went off watch."

"Ah. I see." I took a sip of the steaming coffee. "How far are we from George Town?"

"Two hours. We should make the harbor entrance about eight o'clock. I checked when I put the coffee on. When should we call Aaron?"

"We may as well wait until we're a half-hour out. He just wants to give us their latest guess on where Grissom's meeting is. As crowded as it will be in Elizabeth Harbour, we won't have much choice about where we anchor. We'll just have to take the inflatable to wherever Grissom is."

"Okay. Did you think any more about what we talked about?"

"You mean about how they didn't need a data center to do what O'Hanlon and Dailey were doing?"

"Yes," Mary said. "About that."

"I did. What you said makes sense."

"Then what are they up to?"

"I don't have any evidence to support it, but one idea kept popping into my mind."

"What idea?"

"The Russians."

"Lavrov?" Mary asked.

"Or whatever his real name is. It doesn't matter. Suppose he's not just a gangster; suppose he's working for the Russian government?"

"To smuggle drugs into the U.S.? I guess they would be happy enough to increase our problems."

"That could be just a side benefit. Maybe what they really want is O'Hanlon's network of corrupt politicians and bureaucrats. Think about it. Once Lavrov completes his takeover of O'Hanlon's organization, he has control of a large segment of our government. Why fight a war when you can get what you want for a few dollars?"

"You really think that could be his motive?"

"Look at all the effort they put into trying to manipulate the last election, Mary."

"But there's still a lot of debate over whether that really happened."

"Well, there's a lot of debate, but most of it's about how effective the Russian's efforts were, not on whether they tried to mess up the process. Neither side is arguing that Russian intervention is a good thing."

"So you think Lavrov's out to destabilize our government by paying off corrupt politicians?"

"Paying them off or threatening them with exposure. He wouldn't need them to do anything different from what they were already doing for O'Hanlon, if you think about it. As long as they stay out of his way, he gets what he wants."

"What do you think he wants, Finn?"

"Unfettered access to social media and the news media. He can take it from there, as long as the people in authority keep quiet and don't oppose him."

"You make Lavrov sound like an evil genius."

"Not an evil genius," I said. "I think he's just a tactical operator. He's implementing somebody else's grand plan. There's probably an office in the Kremlin mapping out the strategy for Lavrov to follow."

"What about those data centers?"

"The people in the Kremlin could use them. They could do the things they tried out during the 2016 election, but on a broad scale. This way, all the bogus data would appear to be coming from inside our country. It would be that much more credible, and that much more difficult to blame on outside influence."

"Scary. Not to change the subject, Finn, but I'm starving. You want breakfast?"

"Sure. Am I cooking, or are you?"

"I will. I picked up a half-dozen flying fish off the deck last night. How about scrambled eggs and grits with them?"

"You bet. Nothing like a vixen who cooks."

"Watch yourself; I'll do things to you that even Sylvie Skins wouldn't think of." She gave me a wink as she went down the companionway.

24

"THANKS," I SAID, TAKING MARY'S DISH. "GREAT JOB ON THE flying fish."

"You're welcome. You doing the dishes?"

"Well, it's not like there are many. I was going below for the satellite phone, anyway.

"I made a mess frying the fish. Just put everything in the sink; I'll get it later. We need to call Aaron. I checked the GPS while I was cooking. We've had a favorable current; ETA at the harbor entrance is only 20 minutes from now."

"Okay."

Two minutes later, I was back in the cockpit with the satellite phone. As soon as it locked on a satellite, it rang, surprising us.

"Aaron?"

"Yeah, Finn. I've had this thing auto-dialing you for the last couple of hours."

"Sorry we had the phone turned off. What's up?"

"Mary with you?"

"Hi, Aaron. I'm here."

"Good. First, we narrowed the possibilities for their location down to two places. I'll send a text with the GPS coordinates when we hang up, but both are private islands. They're not too far apart; both in that string of barrier islands between the harbor and Exuma Sound, okay?"

"Okay," I said. "Do they have names?"

"Yeah. One is Fowl Cay. It's a high end, super-exclusive resort. They only book one party at a time. It's worth a look.

"The other place is called Dogfish Cay. It's a little farther offshore from Great Exuma Island, and it's supposed to be uninhabited. It looks uninviting from the satellite images — some ruins from the 18th century, back when the loyalists escaped from what had been the Colonies. Some of them set up shop down there, with slaves, plantations, the whole works. They didn't exactly prosper, I guess, but they built big houses.

"Dogfish Cay's not big enough to have supported agriculture, plus it's rough, craggy, coral rock. I'm not sure what the attraction was for the people who settled there. Maybe they were pirates; there were plenty of them down there. Dogfish Cay would have been easy to defend, too.

"But here's the thing. There are signs of recent activity there. There are also heat signatures on the thermal surveys that don't belong there. Some from people, others from engines — like generators.

"Word is out among the locals that there's been boat traffic around there at night recently. Not local boats. The local fishermen have started giving the place a wide berth; they think somebody's using it as a transshipment point for smuggling — drugs, weapons, maybe even human trafficking. They're scared to get too close. And to top it off, the Bahamian authorities deny that anything unusual is going on out there. That's a sure sign somebody's paying them to look the other way.

"My bet is you'll find our targets on Dogfish Cay, but check out Fowl Cay first. It'll be easier to do, and since it's a business operation, you don't have to be overly sneaky about it. If you go near Dogfish Cay in daylight, everybody in the neighborhood will hear about it.

"Once you've ruled out Fowl Cay, that only leaves Dogfish Cay. You need to wait for the cover of darkness to check it out any closer than binocular distance. Getting ashore will be tough, too. There's no beach; the entire perimeter is steep, with sharp, broken coral. There's a crumbling pier on the side close to Great Exuma, but it will be a swim and climb operation. If there's somebody there up to no good, they'll be watching that pier. Questions so far?"

"Yes. We'll need wetsuits for that. Think you can get some to us in George Town? That kind of thing's hard to come by down there."

"Everything you'll need is already in *Isabella's* lazarette. I should have told you; sorry. Guess I had too much on my mind."

"That's okay; when we discovered there were no provisions aboard, we just assumed we were on our own for supplies in general."

"Yeah. We ran out of time. Figured you could feed yourselves, but the other stuff would be harder to find. We stashed the wetsuits and snorkel gear there before you got to Nassau. There are a few other things that'll come in handy for your mission, too. Also, Mike said to tell you to open the inspection plates on the sides of the centerboard trunk. You'll want to do it with the board down, because there's not much clearance between the board and the trunk. He keeps stashes of weapons and ammo in flat neoprene envelopes fastened inside the trunk — two on each side of the board. You'll find them by reaching down into the trunk."

"Great. Sounds like that's everything we'll need," I said. "Thanks, Aaron."

"Hold on. We're not done. Your mission's gotten a little more complicated."

"Oh, good. I was thinking we might get bored."

"No worries on that score. Pay attention, now."

"Okay. Lay it on us."

"We're well into the analysis of the traffic associated with that server farm at Grissom's place. We still don't know what was on the servers, but we've picked up two important things. One is that the data center was mirrored. There's another data center somewhere that duplicates the functionality of the one at Grissom's. We're working on finding it; it appears to be functional, still. That's something else to ask Grissom and company about."

"Got it. You said two things."

"Yeah. The second one is super important. There's a PC down there in the place where the meeting is being held. We need for you to capture it, intact, and we need the person who is using it, also intact. That PC was controlling the server farm. It's probably the one that wiped the data. You still with me?"

"Yes. Sounds simple enough in concept, but it may be tough to do. The PC isn't likely to be a big challenge, but figuring out who uses it and keeping him alive — that may be a different story."

"Yeah, well you need to do both. The PC will probably be a high-powered, custom-built laptop, like gamers use. If we don't miss our guess, it will have the latest biometric security features, too. It will unlock with facial recognition and fingerprints, more than likely. Probably with a passcode required in addition. We won't be able to crack it without the owner's presence, and it's the only way we'll be able to get into that mirrored data center. You understand what I'm saying?"

"Yes."

"Questions?"

"Yes. Once we have the person and his computer, what are we supposed to do with them?"

"Good that you asked. Here's the biggest change in your mission. You're to capture Grissom, the PC owner, and anyone besides Grissom's peers. Waste the security people, waste Grissom's peers — Stringfellow, Theroux, and Cruz, for sure are there, but — "

"Who is Cruz?" Mary asked. "That's a new name."

"Sorry. I forgot we didn't put him on your target list earlier with the others. He's the honcho for Lavrov's Miami operation. Marco Cruz. What I was about to say is that we need to interrogate the others — Grissom, plus any other attendees besides Grissom's peers. His peers are expendable. Grissom is the priority, because he's the one who has a data center in his backyard. If you waste the others, so be it. Got it?"

I looked over at Mary. She frowned and shook her head. I shrugged.

"That may be a tall order, Aaron," I said. "Wiping them out is what we're good at, but taking prisoners is a different thing."

"Understood. I pointed that out to Mike and Bob when they briefed me. They said they have the utmost confidence that you two are the best ones for the job. Do what you have to do, but keep in mind that the PC geek, Grissom, and any unknowns are more important than the other drug bosses. Especially the unknowns — if Lavrov's not there, he'll have someone there to represent him. We don't think he'll be there in person, so we need to interrogate his representative."

"You keep saying we," Mary said. "That's Finn and me and who else? What are the two of us supposed to do with the prisoners once we have them? You want us to question them?"

"I was coming to that. Once you're in control, call me. We're on our way down there; we have a research vessel with a helicopter already in the vicinity. By late afternoon, I'll be aboard with a specialized interrogation team. When you give me the word, we'll swoop in and take the prisoners off your hands. By the way, don't assume the computer person is a male. We don't know that. Got it?"

"Yes," we both said.

"Anything else from either of you?"

"Yes," Mary said. "We'll recognize Grissom, Stringfellow, and Theroux from our briefing earlier, but you need to send us pictures of Cruz."

"On the way as soon as we disconnect. What else?"

"Finn and I have been kicking ideas around. We think Lavrov's more than just a Russian mobster taking over O'Hanlon's operation. There's too much that doesn't fit that scenario."

"Uh-huh," Aaron said. "I agree, but can you be more specific? What doesn't fit, in your view?"

"The data centers, mainly. O'Hanlon and Dailey were running their whole operation on the back of an envelope, almost. Even with the stuff they had on the corrupt officials and the finances for their activities, everything was on the thumb drive I stole from the Daileys' safe. So why do they need data centers?"

"Yes. That's where we came out, as well. We think this is a Russian government operation aimed at taking over O'Hanlon's network of crooked officials. The scope of their intentions goes beyond just running drugs and human trafficking."

Mary and I exchanged glances, but before either of us could speak, Aaron continued.

"We're doing homework on Lavrov, or whoever he really is. He's a mobster, all right, with a KGB background. He could well be working for a successor organization — FSB, or another Russian intelligence group we haven't discovered yet. He's a high-level operator, but still just a soldier. A general, maybe, if you want to think of him that way, but he's not the one making policy.

"Somebody up the line is calling the shots on this data-center business. Once they get their hooks into O'Hanlon's network, Lavrov's job will probably be to run the criminal side of things. That's a great distraction to cover their other activities, and it generates the cash to pay for everything."

"That's about where Finn and I came out."

"Great minds, and all that," Aaron said. "I planned to save that for later, but since you figured it out, you should know that the person with the PC isn't part of Lavrov's operation. That's our best guess, anyhow. We can't prove it yet, but it looks like that person answers to a chain of command that's parallel to Lavrov's. They both end in Moscow, though. So now you know why we want that person intact. Same goes for Lavrov, of course, but we don't think you'll find him there."

"Why would the person with the PC be there?" Mary asked. "I would think he'd be as leery of getting caught as Lavrov would be."

"Good question. Maybe that person has a cover that makes them appear unimportant. And Lavrov knows we're looking for him, but the computer person still thinks they're invisible. Anything else?"

Mary and I traded glances and shook our heads.

"No, we're at the harbor entrance. It's time for us to go find a spot to anchor," I said. "Send us those GPS coordinates and the photos of Cruz."

"Soon as I hang up," Aaron said. "See you soon. Check in with us before you attack, so we can be on standby. Figure we'll be there in ten minutes after you give us the all-clear."

"Will do," I said, disconnecting the call.

"Shall we douse the sails and take her in under power?" Mary asked. "That dogleg entrance channel looks tight on the chart."

"Might as well," I said. "The anchorage will be extra crowded, too. Fire up the diesel; I'll take care of the sails as soon as you're ready."

25

A LITTLE OVER AN HOUR AFTER OUR CONVERSATION WITH AARON, we were at anchor in Elizabeth Harbour. After threading our way through the hundreds of anchored boats in Stocking Harbour and Elizabeth Harbour, we found a spot half-a-mile southwest of Fowl Cay. We were sitting in the cockpit, scanning our surroundings with the binoculars.

"I've never seen so many boats in one place," Mary said, passing me the binoculars. "I had no idea it would be like this. Why are they all here?"

I shrugged as I took the binoculars. "George Town's been a magnet for cruising boats for a long time. It's a jumping-off place for people headed for the Caribbean who don't want to sail offshore. You can island-hop your way here from the States without ever sailing overnight. Same for people northbound from the Caribbean islands.

"It's a pain in the neck, but if you're too timid to sail offshore or in the dark, it works, I guess. But once you leave here going south, you've got a couple of overnight legs to contend with, so people sit here waiting for perfect conditions.

And you rarely get perfect conditions. A lot of them end up sitting here until it's time for them to go back to the States. George Town's often called Chicken Harbor, because it's where the faint of heart turn around and go home."

"But there must be hundreds of boats here, Finn."

"That's no exaggeration," I said. "In a typical winter, you can find four or five hundred boats crammed in here."

"Why would Lavrov pick this kind of place for a meeting?"

"I can't answer that. Maybe because it's remote, and visitors don't stand out. With all the cruising boats here, the visitors far outnumber local people for a lot of the year. Plus, if you want easy access to and from places where laws are lax, this fits the bill."

"Like where?"

"Haiti, the Dominican Republic, Cuba, some other, smaller island nations. Take your pick. There are plenty of countries close by where money can buy anything you can imagine. This part of the world is a smuggler's dream — has been, for centuries."

"What do you think about Fowl Cay?" Mary asked.

Raising the binoculars to my eyes, I studied the part of Fowl Cay's shoreline that was visible from our perspective. There was a sturdy-looking dock with a gazebo on the end. A fancy launch with a canvas canopy was tied alongside. I watched as a uniformed crewman helped a young couple with two children get aboard. When they were seated, he cast off the dock lines and motored away toward town.

"Looks innocent enough," I said. "A family with two kids just left for George Town in a touristy-looking launch. I would guess it belongs to the resort."

"I saw it tied up there," Mary said. "The operator was talking with another man, both wearing white Bermuda shorts and starched white shirts with epaulets. Think we should waste our time going over there to check it out?"

I thought about that for a few seconds. "We don't exactly have a lot to do between now and nightfall. You never know what we might learn. Plus, it gives us a reason to get a little closer to Dogfish Cay."

"That's so. We're a little far from Dogfish Cay to make out much detail ashore, but it doesn't look inviting. Like Aaron said, lots of sharp coral rock, and no sandy spots to land."

"Let's break out the dinghy and get it put together," I said. "Then we'll unpack the care package Aaron's people left for us and see what's there."

"All right. Sounds good to me. Guess I have to stand up."

"Yep. The dinghy's under your seat. You tired?"

"No, I'm okay. Just being lazy. Someday, I hope we can sail somewhere and hang out, just for the fun of it, you know? Like all these other people here."

"Yes, I know. We should make that happen. But first, we have to catch some crooks."

She opened the locker under the cockpit seat, and we dragged out a green nylon duffle bag. I wrestled it up onto the foredeck while she took three varnished plywood floorboards from the locker. Snapped together, they would give us a firm, flat surface in what would otherwise amount to an oversized inner tube with a fabric bottom.

I opened the bag and found a foot-operated, bellows-type pump with an attached hose on top. Setting it aside, I upended the bag, grabbing it by the bottom and shaking it until the rolled-up gray mass of the deflated dinghy slid out onto the deck.

Unrolling the dinghy, I attached the pump's hose to one of the two inflation valves and stood up. I worked the pump with my foot until the dinghy's forward air chamber began to fill. While it was still soft and wrinkled, I called out to Mary to bring the floorboards. We positioned them in the dinghy's bottom, and I resumed pumping.

"Did you see a bracket in the locker for the outboard?" I asked.

"So that's what that thing is. Yes, now that you say that, I can see how it works, but I was flummoxed by it. You need it now?"

"Bring it up here, yes. It's easier to get it to slide into place before all the fabric is stretched tight."

With the bow section of the dinghy full of air, I disconnected the pump's hose and closed the inflation valve on the dinghy. By the time I hooked the hose up and started filling the dinghy's aft air chamber, Mary was back with the bracket.

"Those four black tapered pins with the blunt points slip into those hard-rubber mounts," I said, as Mary stood, puzzling over how to attach the bracket.

"Aha! I see."

She squatted down and slipped the bracket into place while I continued to work the foot pump. In a few minutes, the dinghy was ready to launch. I tied its bow line to the nearest lifeline stanchion, and we lifted it over the lifelines, letting it slide into the water.

"I've only seen pictures of fold-up inflatables," she said. "It looks like an elongated doughnut."

"It does," I chuckled. "I've heard them called doughnut dinghies. They're not as popular nowadays. Everybody wants rigid, hard-bottom inflatables with big outboards, so they can zoom from place to place at 25 miles an hour. These old ones have their drawbacks, but they're easy to stow on a small boat."

"There are oars in the cockpit locker," she said.

"Good. Stick them in the dinghy while I get the outboard."

I mounted the little outboard. After two pulls on the starter rope, it sputtered to life.

"That was a lot quicker and easier than launching a rigid inflatable," Mary said. "Didn't even need a hoist for that little engine."

"No, but it will be slow — probably four or five miles an hour. It is convenient, and it stows out of the way. This is the way things used to be, back in a simpler time."

"You don't have a big outboard for the dinghy on *Island Girl*."

"No. I like to keep things simple."

"But you have a rigid inflatable. Why?"

"It's more rugged. Besides, these old doughnut dinghies are hard to find down island. Most people want the other kind. Mike probably ordered this one from somewhere in the States. Let's see what kind of goodies Aaron's folks left us."

"Before we go to Fowl Cay?" Mary asked.

"Yes. I think we should put the snorkeling gear in the dinghy. Did you look at the harbor chart for the water around Fowl Cay and Dogfish Cay?"

"Not beyond what I needed to bring *Isabella* into the anchorage. Why?"

"There are coral heads scattered pretty densely along a line from the southeast corner of Fowl Cay. They go almost all the way to Dogfish Cay, in fairly shallow water. After we go to Fowl Cay, we can snorkel our way through the coral and pretend we're looking for lobster. Gives us a reason to get closer to Dogfish Cay."

"Looking for lobster? Like to eat?"

"Yes, like that."

"How do you catch them?"

"Simple. You just dive and grab. They'll dart into holes in the coral, so we'll need sticks to poke them out."

"You think we'll catch any?"

"I don't know, Mary. That's not the point. It's just for cover, okay?"

"But I would love fresh lobster for dinner. That would be so cool, like eating flying fish from on the deck for breakfast."

"Well, maybe we'll get lucky."

"That would be nice, too," Mary said, leering and giving me a wink.

"Let's unpack our snorkel gear and get going, Vixen." That got a lascivious chuckle from her, but she led the way back to the cockpit and opened the lazarette locker.

26

THERE WAS A MAN IN A WHITE UNIFORM TINKERING WITH AN outboard engine in the shade of the gazebo on the Fowl Cay dock. Mary and I let the dinghy coast to a stop against the dock near him. He looked over at us and smiled, walking over and squatting down to talk with us.

"Good day. May I help you?" he asked, with the slight British accent common among Bahamians.

"We wondered if the Fowl Cay Resort's restaurant is open to the public," Mary said, smiling up at him.

"Well, sometimes, yes. But only when we are between guests. I'm sorry that's not the case now. We have a large family group staying here for the next week. There are some good places in George Town, though. What kind of food were you looking for? Maybe I can recommend a place."

I opened our little cooler and took out a beer. "Care for one?" I asked.

"I don't mind if I do, thanks," he said, reaching out and taking it from my hand and twisting the top off. "Thank you."

"You're welcome," I said.

"We read about the chef here," Mary said. "He was written up on a travel website."

"Ah, yes. He is famous. And he deserves to be. I'm sorry we can't accommodate you."

"Oh, we understand," Mary said. "But we wanted to ask. We've also heard there are lobster to be found among the coral heads around here. Is that so?"

He smiled as he took a sip of beer. Nodding, he said, "Yes, ma'am, sometimes. Were you wishing to buy? Or to catch?"

"We want to catch them," Mary said. "I'm sure we'll appreciate them more if we have to find them ourselves."

He grinned. "That is so. You may find some. Not too many people try this close to George Town. They think these coral heads are already picked over, you see. So they go far away." He chuckled. "Far away, where everybody else goes. But there are lobster here, yes. You follow the coral heads in the shallows down that way." He pointed toward Dogfish Cay. "But don't go too close to that island."

"Dogfish Cay?" Mary asked. "Why not? No lobster there?"

He shrugged. "Maybe some are there. My friends used to catch them there, before the people came."

"People?" I asked. "I read that Dogfish Cay was uninhabited."

"It was. But some people came. They stay there now and chase everyone away. So it is best to not go there."

"Did they buy the island or something?" Mary asked.

"No one knows. But the police, they will not do anything. Some of my friends, fishermen, they see boats around the island late at night. Not local boats. They think maybe the narco traffickers are using it. Maybe they pay the police? I don't know, but it is best not to find out, I think."

"We heard there were ruins there, from the American

colonists who came here in the late 1700s, after the revolution. We wanted to explore them. There's one big house in particular that we read about."

"Yes, I know that place. The story is it belonged to a pirate. But you cannot go there now. That is where the bad people are. There are six men, like soldiers. They stay there all the time. Some others, they come and go. The bosses, we think. There are twelve people there now, counting the soldiers."

"How mysterious," Mary said. "How do your friends know all of this?"

The man looked sheepish for a moment, and then said, "Girls. Sometimes when the bosses are not there, the soldiers will go into George Town, to the bars. And they are looking for girls, you know? Not nice girls."

"Oh," Mary said. "So they tell the girls things to impress them?"

"Yes, and sometimes, they take some girls back to the island for a few days." He shook his head. "And then the girls, they tell their friends about how these men are living in that big house. They have fixed up some rooms for the bosses. Very nice, the girls say. The soldiers, they live in another building — what used to be the kitchen and servants' quarters, back in the old days."

"This is so fascinating," Mary said. "Like a book, or a movie. How exciting!"

"No, not exciting. Dangerous. These men are bad people. And except when they take the girls there, nobody from here is allowed to go there. This makes many of us angry, that they have taken over the island. But these men, they have guns. They have made threats to the girls, about talking, and to fishermen who come too near. You must stay away from there."

"Thank you for warning us, then. We will definitely stay

away from Dogfish Cay. But there are other loyalist ruins we can explore, aren't there?"

"Yes, ma'am." He pointed over our heads. "Some on Man O' War Cay, some on Crab Cay. All safe to go to. But not Dogfish Cay."

"Well, thank you so much for your help," Mary said. "We should go see if we can catch some lobster for dinner."

"It was my pleasure to visit with you, and thank you for the beer. I hope you find many lobster."

"Thanks," I said, as I started the outboard and pulled away from the dock.

We skirted the Fowl Cay shoreline until we reached the island's northeast point. I steered northeast for a few more yards until we were in the midst of the coral heads. Then I shut the outboard down.

"Shall I drop the anchor?" Mary asked.

"No, let's put our gear on and get in the water. I'll tow the dinghy as we snorkel; there's not enough wind to give me any trouble with it blowing around."

27

WE TOOK OUR TIME, DRIFTING ALONG ON THE SURFACE AND watching the coral landscape beneath us. The water was between six and ten feet deep, shallower over the coral heads. The bottom between the coral heads was sandy, with broken pieces of coral and occasional patches of weed. Mary dove periodically to get a close look at the shells on the bottom, or to study the sides of a coral head. The few lobster that we saw were too small to be worth catching.

After about an hour in the water, I put a hand on Mary's leg to get her attention. She stopped kicking and let her feet sink, her head coming out of the water as she looked over at me.

Pulling the snorkel from my mouth, I said, "How about a little break? Let's sit in the dinghy and drink a beer."

"You tired?"

"No. Look over your shoulder."

We were in a patch of coral heads about 150 yards southeast of Dogfish Cay, having drifted well to the southeast from our starting point.

"Oh, I see," she said, putting her hands on the tube of the dinghy.

She scissored her legs, and the thrust of her flippers lifted her into the dinghy. As she rolled to a sitting position, her feet in the water, she removed her flippers and put them in the dinghy. While she worked the strap of her mask free of her hair, I paddled around to the other side of the dinghy and hoisted myself aboard.

"We should drop the anchor this time," I said. "We don't want to drift much closer to Dogfish Cay."

She dropped the little folding anchor, and I took two beers from the cooler. Twisting the top from one, I handed it to her and opened my own.

"Cheers," I said, tilting my bottle toward her.

She clicked the neck of her bottle against mine. "Cheers. Too bad we're not finding dinner."

"It's early, yet, and there are more places to try. Right out there, for instance." I pointed past Dogfish Cay at a small, low-lying island. "That's Whelk Cay."

Mary shifted her position, moving to sit beside me, so we were both facing Dogfish Cay. "Whelk? Like the sea snails?"

"Right."

"They're edible, aren't they?"

"Yes. But I'd rather have lobster. Or almost anything else."

"Why? You don't like whelk?"

"They're okay, I guess. I don't like the texture. Too chewy to suit me."

"Like conch?"

"Sort of. You see the guy on Dogfish Cay checking us out?"

"Yes." She turned toward me, putting her arms around my neck and giving me a lingering kiss.

When we came up for air, she said, "Think we were convincing enough?"

"I don't know about him, but you fooled me. For a minute there, I thought I might get lucky."

"Later, maybe." Smiling, she turned toward the island and took a sip of her beer. "Looks like it worked. He's moved on."

"Yes. Once you attacked me, he put his binoculars away. I mean, he watched for a minute, but I guess he decided the show wasn't worth waiting for. Not enough action to keep his attention."

She elbowed me, hard. I was massaging my ribs when she asked, "Were you watching him that whole time?"

"I thought you were just doing that to provide cover for us. Didn't you mean for me to keep an eye on him?"

"You play the part of a cad all too well, Finn. You old villain, you can forget about getting lucky any time soon."

"Sorry. I thought we were working, anyway."

"Might as well, I suppose." She picked up the binoculars and trained them on Dogfish Cay. "He's about to round the northeast corner. His back's to us, and he's got a rifle slung over his shoulder. Guess our friend at Fowl Cay wasn't exaggerating."

She twisted her torso, sweeping the binoculars from right to left. "There's another one coming around the western side, headed this way. He's armed, too. Those boys are serious." She lowered the binoculars. "Should we move?"

"Wait for this second one to walk the length of this side of the island," I said, "and let's time him. If we see the first one reappear on the northwest corner about the time this one rounds the southeast corner, we'll know they have two men on watch. Or if we see a third, that's worth knowing, too. That'll come in handy tonight. Then we can move up to Whelk Cay and get a look at the island from the other side."

Mary lifted her binoculars again, studying the shoreline of Dogfish Cay for several seconds. "I missed it before; I was too focused on the sentry. There's a pier of sorts about a third of the way across from the left. It's made from the same coral rock as the island, so it's tough to see. I can't tell, but it may enclose a small-boat basin."

Reaching for the binoculars, I took a quick look. "You're right. I saw movement on the other side of it, like maybe a speedboat rising and falling with the swell. It's hidden most of the time; it only pops up on the crests."

"There might be a path from there up to the houses," Mary said.

"Did you see something like that?" I asked.

"No, just guessing. I wonder if that pier is new, or if it's left from the loyalists' days."

"Hard to know. I can't imagine why loyalists would have settled on that lump of rock. Given that most of them were plantation owners, that place looks wrong. Nothing would grow on all that rock."

"There's a bit of scrub," Mary said. "There must be patches of dirt in there. Anyway, the man at Fowl Cay said the rumor was they were pirates."

"I'm not looking forward to picking our way through all that broken coral in the dark," I said.

"Our guy just finished his pass along this side," Mary said. "Thirty minutes. And here comes the first guy, back again. They must be on a path, to be moving as fast as they are."

"You sure it's the same guy coming around again?"

"Yes. Same T-shirt. There are only two of them on watch at a time. Let's go to Whelk Cay."

I nodded and cranked the outboard, steering for the center of Whelk Cay. That took us past the eastern side of Dogfish Cay at a distance of about 150 to 200 yards. The character of Dogfish Cay's shoreline didn't change; it wouldn't be any fun getting ashore tonight. Whelk Cay was a raised sand bar about two hundred yards long, and from my study of the chart, maybe a hundred feet wide at its widest point.

"Let's beach the dinghy," I said, as we approached Whelk Cay.

"All right. Are we going ashore?"

"Yes. It looks like this is mostly sand. We should be able to find a clear spot to beach the dinghy, then we can walk over to the other side. There may be enough of a rise in the middle of the island to give us a little cover. We can lie on the sand looking over the ridge and study Dogfish Cay without being visible."

28

We settled in on the other side of the low ridge of sand and took our time surveying our target. Dogfish Cay was about a third of a mile away. With our elbows on the ground to steady the binoculars, we could make out enough detail for our purposes. From this angle, we could even see the ruins of the big house. It sat just below the crest of the high ground in the middle of Dogfish Cay, so it was hidden from our view earlier. There were people moving around outside under a large canvas awning.

"Strange awning," Mary said. "It looks like it started out white, but it's mottled looking. And those curtains on the sides, they aren't hanging straight down. They're pulled farther out in some places than others and maybe staked to the ground. Looks random. I can see through them in spots, but not everywhere."

I chuckled. "That's camouflage netting. You've never seen it before?"

"No. Guess I missed something, not being in the military, huh?"

"Not enough to worry about. You spotted it; that's what counts."

"It's not doing them much good, if we can see it, is it?"

"It's there to foil satellite surveillance or aerial photography, like from the balloons and drones the DEA use. From a distance, it breaks up the straight lines and recognizable patterns."

"So that's why Aaron didn't notice anybody in the satellite photos," Mary said. "How many people do you count under the awning?"

"Six. Did you get a count?"

"Yes. The same. That would be Grissom, Stringfellow, Theroux, and their counterpart from Miami. Plus two others. You think they might be part of the security force? The two extras?"

"Maybe," I said. "Our friend on Fowl Cay said there were six guards. Two are on duty. If they work eight hours a day in two four-hour watches, that means two would be asleep. The other two would be doing whatever they do to pass the time. It could be two of them, but I doubt the hired help would mingle with the big shots. You think they would?"

"No. Just checking," Mary said. "That smaller building off to the right with the covered walkway to the big house must be the servants' quarters the man in Fowl Cay mentioned. The covered walkway was a standard thing back when they put the kitchen in a separate structure. Kept the rain off the food when the servants brought it to the dining room."

"Yeah," I said. "And the guy on the dock said there were six guests there. So that means Lavrov's deputy and the computer geek Aaron mentioned are with Grissom and his pals right now."

"The computer geek — I wonder why he's hanging out

with the bosses," Mary said. "The other one's probably Lavrov's second in command. Sergei, last name unknown. No surprise that he's mixing with the honchos. But I'm not sure about the computer geek. He should be hiding in a dark corner playing video games. I wouldn't expect him to be socializing with Grissom and the boys."

"Why do you say that?" I asked.

"If O'Hanlon was running his operation on the back of an envelope, I don't think the data centers have anything to do with drug smuggling and human trafficking. So there would be no reason for the computer nerd to mingle with the mob types. But then why even bring him here?" Mary asked.

I shrugged. "Security, maybe. It's a safe place to keep him. And it's outside the States, but close enough if he needs to get there in a hurry."

"How do you suppose he's communicating?"

"A broadband satellite connection would be my guess," I said. "That type of gear is small and portable, these days. Small enough so he could move it inside during the daytime, out of sight of any aerial surveillance."

"So, what do you think, Finn? Seen enough?"

"We've seen about all we're going to. You ready to go back to *Isabella*?"

"Yes. It's going to be a long night; we should rest while we can."

"I'm for that. We'll need to check in with Aaron later, but we should have a rough plan worked out before we call him. Let's go home and take a long nap. We'll figure out how to do this when we're fresh."

Two hours later, I woke from my nap. Mary was still asleep. It was mid-afternoon, time to figure out how we were going to carry out our mission. I filled the coffee pot and put it on the stove. Mary woke up as the coffee finished percolating.

"Yes," she said, rolling to a sitting position on the settee where she napped. She rubbed her eyes.

"Yes?" I asked, with a chuckle. "Yes what?"

"Yes, I'd love a cup of coffee. Didn't you offer me one just now?"

"No, but I was about to wake you up."

"Guess I dreamed it, then. Must have been the aroma."

I filled a mug and handed it to her, pouring another one for myself. As I filled the thermos, I asked, "Ready to make some plans?"

"Sure," she said, taking a sip of her coffee. "We're going to swim in, right?"

"Yes. There's no other way to be sure somebody won't spot the dinghy."

"That's where I came out, too. But where will we leave it? You're not thinking we'll swim from here, are you?"

"No. We can take it out to Whelk Cay again."

"Why there, instead of among the coral heads off Fowl Cay? That would be closer."

"It would be a little closer," I said, "but they'll be less likely to expect an attack coming from the Exuma Sound side of the island."

"That's a good point," Mary said, scrunching up her brow.

"Why the frown, then?"

"The speedboat in that basin behind the pier."

"What about it?" I asked.

"We should disable it, to be sure nobody uses it to escape. You know — just in case something goes wrong."

"You're right. Got an idea of how to manage that?"

"Well, I like the idea of attacking from the offshore side, but — "

"Wait," I said. "I've been assuming we were going to swim in together."

"Me, too. You have a different idea?"

"Well, maybe. We've got those earwig radios from Aaron's care package. We could split up and still coordinate our attack."

"Okay. With radios and the night-vision goggles, I feel like this is some sci-fi game. I'm not used to having stuff like that. But go ahead. What are you thinking?"

"Well, the NVGs will play a part, too. What if we took the dinghy straight to those last coral heads out to the southeast of Fowl Cay — the ones where we were closest to Dogfish Cay?"

"You mean the ones where you thought you were going to get lucky?"

"Yes, those." I smiled.

"Okay, we anchor it there? But that's not on the side where you wanted to land."

"No it's not. But we won't anchor there. I wasn't factoring in all the high-tech goodies Aaron left us. We can hang out in that spot with the thermal imaging scope and wait until one of the guards has walked past the pier. It took him about 30 minutes to walk from the northwest point to the southeast point, and the pier's in the middle, roughly. Okay?"

"Okay," Mary said.

"So a few minutes before he passes the pier, I'll start swimming. I won't be able to use the NVGs in the water, but you can keep watch and call me on the earwig; they're waterproof, and I'll be on the surface, so I'll have reception. We'll time it so that I get to the basin just after he passes it. That will give me around ten minutes to work before the next guard comes around the northwest point. Still with me?"

"Yes."

"Once I'm in the basin, you take off and run straight over to Whelk Cay and beach the dinghy. Meanwhile, I'll disable the speedboat that's in the basin and set up an ambush for the guard. You'll be swimming to the offshore side of Dogfish Cay. We'll stay in touch on the radios to make sure we have the timing right, but what we want to do is hit both guards at the same time. That way, there's less chance they'll raise an alarm."

"But what if our timing's off, Finn? I'm not sure I'll have time to land the dinghy and swim in that fast."

"That's the beauty of the radios. If you're delayed for some reason, I'll just wait and let my guard pass me by. When you're in position, we'll get another chance to hit them at the same time — or close enough."

Mary grinned. "I like it. I was worried about that anyway, when I thought we were swimming in together. How were we going to nail both guards before one of them figured out something was wrong? Problem solved. So we take them out, then meet up at the servants' quarters?"

"Yes. We slip in and kill the four remaining guards, and then move to the big house. If we wait until early morning, everybody should be asleep, and we can take them one at a time."

"Nothing to it," Mary said. "I like it. Shall we call Aaron and fill him in?"

"Yes. Let's go up in the cockpit so the phone can acquire a signal. You bring the thermos; I'll get the phone."

29

It was a little after midnight as Mary and I sat in the dinghy, watching for the guard to come around the corner of Dogfish Cay.

When we called Aaron after our nap earlier in the afternoon, we discussed our plan with him. After a little back and forth, we agreed that he should expect our call for the pickup of our captives sometime between one and three a.m. Aaron reported that the research vessel was holding steady just over the horizon to the northeast — a few minutes' flying time for the helicopter that was aboard.

Finished with the call, we went through the equipment that was now in our waterproof belt packs. For several minutes, we tested the earwig radios, subvocalizing to take advantage of the throat microphones. With a bit of practice, we learned to communicate without speaking aloud, letting the little gadgets relay our thoughts almost without audible speech.

We alternated between resting and refining our plans until midnight, then we got in the dinghy and came out here. Now

Mary was watching Dogfish Cay with a thermal imaging scope as we drifted slowly over the coral heads where we hunted lobster earlier.

Our night-vision goggles were in our belt packs, along with Glock 19s and two extra, fully loaded magazines each. We also had suppressors for the pistols, but we would affix them once we were ashore on Dogfish Cay. We each had two flash/bang grenades in our belt packs, and razor-sharp commando knives with knuckle-guard grips were strapped to our calves.

"Here comes the guard," Mary said. "You ready?"

"Ready. See you at the servants' quarters."

I put on my flippers and mask and slipped into the water as she started the outboard and headed for Whelk Cay. The surface of the water was calm with the barrier islands between me and Exuma Sound, so I made good time. I stopped often and raised my head to make sure I was on course.

Reaching the outside of the pier that enclosed the little boat basin, I found a handhold and checked my watch. I was ahead of schedule. The guard would only be about halfway between the point and the pier; I had time to kill.

Done with my mask and flippers, I took them off and clipped them to my belt for the moment. Feeling around with my free hand, I found a few loose, fist-sized rocks. I used them to weight the mask and flippers, ensuring that they would sink right away.

Freed of the snorkeling gear, I worked my way to the corner of the pier. I found a shallow shelf and crouched there. With my knees on the shelf, I took out the night-vision goggles and put them on, watching for the guard.

I no sooner spotted him than he stopped. He was opposite my position, staring out across the basin as he fumbled to open a pocket on his cargo shorts. I turned off the NVGs and let them hang around my neck. Now that I knew he was there, I could see him without the NVGs; he was a darker shadow against the backdrop of the island. Then he lit a cigarette.

Hoping he wasn't planning to stand there until he finished it, I settled in to wait. Luck was with me. He put his lighter and the cigarette pack in his pocket and resumed walking. I gave him ten minutes, and then I swam into the basin. The boat we saw earlier was the only one in there. It was a ski-boat about 16 feet long with two big outboard engines.

I climbed aboard and removed the shroud from the first engine. Feeling my way, I found the high voltage wire from the ignition coil to the distributor and yanked it out, tossing it over the side. I put the shroud back on that engine and repeated the process with the other one. Nobody would leave the island in this boat. Not tonight, anyway,

Checking my watch, I saw that the guard had been gone from the basin for 15 minutes. He should be rounding the southeast corner of the island now. I called Mary on the radio, subvocalizing, letting the throat microphone do its work.

"Vixen," Mary answered.

"Boat is disabled. Waiting on my target."

"Copy that. Me, too."

"Soon, Vixen. Villain out."

"Copy, Villain. Vixen out."

We were fortunate with our timing. We wouldn't have to wait for the guards to make another round. I put the night-vision goggles on again and crept along the side of the pier, staying low. As we guessed, there was a footpath running along the shoreline. I crossed it and found a rocky outcropping big enough to hide behind. I dropped into a crouch, putting the mass of the rock between me and the guard's approach. Taking my commando knife from its sheath, I threaded the fingers of my right hand through the knuckle guard and relaxed.

I smelled the guard before I heard him. Another smoker. I loosened up my muscles as best I could, waiting. About a minute later, he strolled past me, cigarette in hand, his face turned toward the water. I lurched to my feet, lunging toward him from behind, my left hand catching his left shoulder as I smashed the knuckle guard into the side of his head. That may have killed him, but I wouldn't chance it.

Reaching over his shoulder, I caught his chin with my left hand before he collapsed. I pulled him back against me and drove the point of the knife into the right side of his neck, the blade passing behind his jugular vein and his throat. Holding the knife rigid in my hand, I thrust it forward, letting the cutting edge do its job. The knife sliced through muscle, veins, and cartilage. I wiped it on the right shoulder of his shirt and let him fall as I returned the knife to its sheath.

"Vixen," I subvocalized, planning to update Mary.

She didn't answer. I began walking, remembering the satellite image of the island with its paths that Aaron sent us earlier. I would be at the servants' quarters in a few minutes. Mary was either dead, or her target was too close for her to risk answering me. I would know soon, one way or the other.

I began counting off the seconds to keep myself focused as I followed a footpath up the rocky hill. One minute and 50 seconds later, I heard Mary.

"Villain, Vixen."

"Copy. On my way to the rendezvous. Villain out."

"Copy. Me too. Vixen out."

I sighed with relief and kept moving. As I walked, I took the pistol from my waterproof belt pack and attached the suppressor. I slipped the pistol into the empty holster at my waist.

Our plan was to dispatch as many of our targets as we could without using the pistols. Even with a suppressor, the sound of a shot from a nine-millimeter pistol could wake a light sleeper. Still, it was best to be ready for a gunfight if one came our way.

Soon, the slope of the hill became less steep. I could make out the top of the roof on the big house, just coming into view over the rocks as I neared the crest of the hill. Once on level ground, I dropped to a crouch and got my bearings. The back of the big house was a hundred yards in front of me. To the left and a little closer to me, I saw the servants' quarters with the covered walkway connecting it to the big house. There were no lights showing in either of the buildings. As I began to creep toward the servants' quarters, I saw Mary coming up the slope from the opposite side.

"Vixen," I subvocalized.

"Got you in sight, Villain."

30

WE MET AT THE WALL ON THE NORTHEAST END OF THE SERVANTS' quarters, as we had planned earlier. I noticed that Mary's pistol was in her holster with the suppressor attached. We nodded at each other and turned away, Mary to work her way along the front wall of the low building while I went around the back wall. Meeting her at the entrance under the covered walkway, I took the lead.

Peering into the open doorway, I saw a large open area to the right that was the original kitchen. It still served that purpose; there were modern gas appliances against one wall. To the immediate left of the entrance, there was a wall that must separate living quarters from the work space. About halfway along the wall, roughly 20 feet from me, there was a dark, shadowy area, an archway leading into the living quarters.

I pointed at it, and Mary nodded and moved to a position on this side of the opening with her back against the wall. Right behind her, I dropped to the floor and slithered to a spot that allowed me to peer through the opening. There was a

single, large room, like a dormitory or a barracks. Six single
beds were aligned along the back wall. Four of them were
occupied.

Although we thought we might find an arrangement like
this, it was our worst-case scenario. When we made our plans,
we hoped that we would find the guards in individual or
double-occupancy rooms. With four men sleeping in the same
small space, it was unlikely that we could kill all of them
before at least one woke up.

Creeping across the opening with my belly an inch or two
off the floor, I reached the other side. Standing with my back
to the wall, I looked across the opening at Mary. She nodded,
and I raised four fingers on my right hand, closed my fist, and
then raised one finger. That was our prearranged signal to
indicate four men in one room. She nodded again.

Closing my fist and holding it at eye level, I raised one
finger at a time at one-second intervals. When I raised the
third finger, we squeezed through the opening. She went left
and I went right.

My first target was asleep on his right side, his back to me. I
drove my commando knife into his left kidney. He gasped, and
I pulled his pillow over his head, muffling his moan. Twisting
the knife vigorously to do maximum damage, I held him still
until I was sure he was gone.

Mary's man was asleep on his back, snoring softly. Just as I
drove my knife into my man's kidney, she put the heel of her
left hand against her victim's chin, forcing his head back. She
put her weight behind a thrust that drove her blade in under
his chin and up through his soft palate into his brain. It was a
good choice, given his position, but it caused him to convulse.
His thrashing woke the other two.

I vaulted over the first man I killed. The next one was just getting out of bed when I smashed the knuckle guard of my knife into the side of his head. He fell back, unconscious, and I cut his throat. Mary's second man pulled a pistol from under his pillow before she was within striking distance of him. Holding the pistol in his right hand, he racked the slide with his left, chambering a round.

She tugged at her knife, but she couldn't free it from her first victim. It cost her a second or two to get her fingers free of the knuckle guard, giving the man with the pistol time to point it at her. With her hand free of the knuckle guard, she turned to face him. Her eyes wide, she raised her hands in surrender and stuck her tongue out at him.

While he was distracted by her antics, I struck him from behind, going for his right kidney with my commando knife. He gasped and whirled before I could drive my knife home. I cut him, but not badly enough to slow him down. Stepping back, I grabbed his pistol with my left hand.

By forcing the slide back, I rendered it incapable of firing as long as I could hold on. He was quick and strong, grabbing my right wrist in a vice-like grip with his left hand. That kept me from using the knife. He struggled to yank the pistol free so he could shoot me.

I was barely holding my own, wrestling with him. Then he yelped and collapsed against me. His weight drove me back against my previous victim's bed. I shoved my assailant away and realized that Mary had her left arm around his throat. She lowered him to the floor and pulled a folding combat knife from his right kidney.

I nodded my thanks, but she was already focused on retrieving her commando knife from her first victim's corpse. She succeeded and wiped it on his bedding. Putting it down for a moment, she folded her other knife and returned it to a sheath on her belt. She picked up the commando knife, laced her fingers through the knuckle guard again, and looked at me. Gesturing toward the opening to the kitchen, she shrugged. I nodded, and she led the way back outside.

"Ready for round two?" she asked, her voice soft.

"Ready."

We followed the walkway into the big house and went through an open doorway into what was once the dining room. There were four good-sized folding tables pushed together to serve as a conference table. Six comfortable-looking chairs were arranged around the table, with several more against one wall. A large, roll-around whiteboard with several dry-erase markers and an eraser in the tray stood against the other wall. The only exit besides the door from the kitchen walkway was through a wide archway.

We went around opposite sides of the table, one of us stopping on each side of the archway and scanning the space beyond. I was thankful for the night-vision goggles as I studied the large center hallway. To my left was the main entrance to the house, which once featured a pair of oversized doors but now was open to the outside. Opposite where we stood, there was another archway that opened into a living room furnished with patio furniture.

About halfway down the hall, there was a wide staircase that led up to a balcony. The balcony was U-shaped, wrapping around three sides of the entrance hall.

I could make out three doors opening onto the opposite side of the balcony. Bedrooms, most likely, and probably replicated on the side of the balcony above our heads.

To my right, toward the back of the house and behind the staircase, there were two more doorways in the opposite wall. These were the first doorways we saw that were equipped with doors, and they were closed. In the back wall of the center hall was another double doorway without doors. It led outside onto a veranda.

I motioned for Mary to cover me. She nodded, and I crept into the hall, facing the back of the house. As I suspected, there were two doorways in the wall on my right, mirroring the two under the staircase. These were hung with doors, as well, and they were closed.

Still careful to move silently, I turned and went into the living room, but only far enough to see that the only access was through the archway behind me. Going back into the hallway, I motioned for Mary to join me.

31

TOGETHER, WE WENT TO THE FIRST DOORWAY IN THE LEFT WALL and took up positions on either side of it. I still gripped my commando knife, but I gestured for Mary to sheath hers and draw her pistol. When she nodded to say she was ready, I reached for the knob on the door and turned it slowly.

The door moved slightly as the bolt was drawn from the strike plate in the door frame. Glad it wasn't locked and praying that the hinges were freshly oiled, I swung the door open and stepped back. Mary and I scanned the parts of the room that we each could see as I took a roll of duct tape from my belt pack.

We gave each other a thumbs-up. There was one person asleep in a single bed. We moved into position, one on each side of the bed, Mary with her pistol trained on the sleeper's head. I reached across him and plastered duct tape over his mouth.

He woke with a start, trying to sit up, but I held him down. Mary put the end of her pistol's suppressor against the bridge of his nose. She shined a keychain flashlight on the pistol. Watching his eyes as he realized what was happening, she said in a soft voice, "Struggle and you die. Cooperate and you live. Blink once if you understand."

He blinked.

"Good boy," she said. "Now we're going to roll you over on your stomach and cuff your wrists and ankles."

I grabbed his right shoulder, and he let me roll him over. I cinched his wrists together behind his back with plasticuffs, pulling them up tight. Moving to the foot of the bed, I cuffed his ankles. Passing a precut, six-foot length of parachute cord through the plasticuffs at his wrists and ankles, I drew it up tight. Having pulled his wrists and ankles together behind his back, I tied the cord. Then I picked up the duct tape and took two wraps around his head, covering his mouth to secure the single piece of tape I used to gag him at first.

We repeated the same steps with the occupants of the other three rooms on the ground floor. It took us no more than five minutes to secure the four men. I led Mary back into the dining/conference room. We needed to regroup. When we made our plans, we didn't consider that some of our targets might be on the second floor of this decrepit old house.

"Recognize them?" I asked.

"Grissom, Stringfellow, Theroux, and Cruz," she said. "You agree?"

"Yes. That leaves our two unknowns upstairs. I hope the stairs don't squeak."

"They're almost 300 years old, Finn. They're bound to squeak. How do you want to do this?"

"The floor upstairs will be noisy, too. Probably worse than the stairs. If we make it up the stairs without waking them, we'll take them the same way we took the others. If one of them wakes up and surprises us, we may have a gunfight on our hands. All we can do is try to keep them alive if that happens."

I paused, but Mary didn't say anything.

"Here's how I see it, then," I said. "I'll go up a couple of steps ahead of you and if one of them hears us and shows his face, I'll punch him out if I can. If not, you shoot him, but try for a non-lethal wound. Then while I deal with the first one, you go after the second. Okay so far?"

"Yes."

"We've got another problem. There are six rooms, but only two people. Even if the stairs don't squeak and we catch the first one by surprise, there's a good chance the second one will hear something."

"Yes. What else are you thinking?" she asked.

"If we're lucky enough to get the first one before one of them wakes up, leave him to me. You go after the second one and hold him at gunpoint until I get there to tie him up. Make sense? Or do you have a different idea?"

"No. Let's go get 'em."

I nodded. "Follow me."

Our worry about the stairs proved to be well-founded. I was a little over halfway up when a man came through one of the doors, a pistol in his right hand. I took the rest of the stairs in two jumps.

"Who's there?" he called, a split second before I was on him.

Grabbing for his pistol with my left hand as I swung for his jaw with the knuckle guard, I missed the pistol and got his right wrist. Mary squeezed past us as he lurched into me. He was stepping inside my punch as he tried to head-butt me.

Letting his momentum push me backward, I avoided the

head-butt and lifted my knee into his groin. He grunted, but kept his focus, jerking his gun hand around, trying to break my grip as he kept pushing me backward. He hooked his foot behind one of my ankles.

I let him trip me, twisting as we fell to avoid ending up underneath him. Trapping the foot he used to trip me between my ankles, I rolled on top of him. I felt his left hand grasp my neck, his thumb going for my larynx. I smashed the knuckle guard of my knife into his left elbow and heard a satisfying crack. His left arm fell away, and I put the point of my knife into his throat just far enough to draw blood.

"Drop the pistol," I said, moving the knife so he could feel it cutting his flesh.

There was a clunk as his weapon hit the floor. Keeping the pressure on my knife, I released his wrist just long enough to shove the pistol away. I grabbed his wrist again and pulled the knife back from his throat so I could land a blow on the point of his chin with the knuckle guard. His eyes rolled back in his head and I felt his body relax.

Scrambling to my knees, I rolled off him and recovered his pistol, pointing it at him, just in case. A flicker of movement caught my attention, and I looked up to see Mary, leaning against the wall, watching me, a grin on her face.

"Good moves, old man. Took you long enough, though."

"You could have helped. How long were you watching?"

"Long enough. You were doing just fine; you didn't need help. I enjoyed the show; I even picked up a few tricks. Just kidding about the old man part. Don't worry; you've still got it."

"Where's the other one, smart-ass?"

"Oh, he's tied up right now. And I found his computer. Shall we call in the clean-up detail?"

"Sure." I took the satellite phone from my belt pack and handed it to her.

"You make the call," I said. "I want to cuff this one before he comes to."

32

MARY AND I SAT IN THE LIVING ROOM OF THE CRUMBLING mansion with Aaron. The helicopter was taking our prisoners back to the research vessel.

"Nice work, you two," Aaron said. "We weren't expecting all six of them to survive."

"You should have said something before you put them all on the chopper," Mary said. "We could have taken care of the rejects for you."

He gave her a long look, his face devoid of emotion. I could tell he was wondering about her mental state, given her recent breakdown. I didn't have any doubts about her, though. Not after tonight. Mary was back, better than ever.

"She's pulling your chain, Aaron," I said. "Don't let her mess with you. It was the luck of the draw. Given that they were sleeping in separate rooms, it was easy enough to capture them. Who knows what your team might get from Grissom's peers?"

"Yeah, you're right. It's a good thing we got Cruz, especially."

"Why Cruz? You've never mentioned him before until right before this mission."

"He never popped up on our radar before. He was just another top-tier distributor, maybe more into human trafficking than the others."

"So that's why you're eager to question him?" Mary asked.

"Well, yes, but also because we just found that second data center, the one that mirrors the one in Jacksonville. It's in Cruz's compound, in Miami. If we move fast enough, we can isolate it from network access. That means they won't be able to wipe it clean. The IT bunch is hard at work on that, right now."

Aaron held the prisoners' passports in his hand. Flipping through them, he pulled out two and set the others aside on the coffee table.

"Nikolai Sergei Popovich," he said, opening one. "Born in Russia, naturalized U.S. citizen. He's the one with the broken arm and the slash on his throat. He put up a fight?"

"Yes," I said. "He and the computer geek were sleeping in two of the upstairs rooms. The stairs aren't in good shape. He woke up, met us with a pistol in his hand."

"You should have seen Finn's moves, Aaron. I'm in awe."

Aaron frowned. "You watched Finn take him down?"

"She's picking on me about being old and slow. She subdued the computer geek while I was mixing it up with Sergei. She still had time to watch the fight."

"Sergei must know what he's doing," Aaron said.

"No kidding," Mary said. "He was vicious; it's a good thing Finn jumped him, all joking aside. I'm not sure I would have survived that one."

"I'll be interested to see what you can learn about him," I

said. "I'd bet he's one of Lavrov's buddies from his *Spetsnaz* days. He's no slouch at hand-to-hand combat."

"Well, we've picked up rumors about him, you know," Aaron said. "Now we may be able to confirm them. With any luck we can find out a little more about Lavrov from Sergei, too."

He put Popovich's passport on the table with the others and opened the one still in his hand. "Gregory David Lewis. Born in New Mexico, U.S.A. But look at all the stamps in this character's passport. Well-traveled. My bet is he's another one who isn't the person he claims to be. You took him, Mary?"

"Yes."

"He give you any trouble?"

"No." She chuckled. "He was sitting up in bed, playing a video game on an iPad when I walked in on him. He took one look at my pistol and wet the bed."

"You serious?"

"I swear. Dropped the iPad and raised his hands. Started crying while I cuffed him. He was as docile as a kitten. I felt sorry for him until I remembered who he was hanging out with. He should crack like an egg once your people start on him."

"You never know," Aaron said. "You just never know. He may be the toughest nut out of the whole bunch."

"What's next on the agenda?" I asked, after several seconds passed in silence.

"The chopper's bringing our forensics team in. We'll go over this place from top to bottom. Once we get enough data to identify the guards you took out, we'll make them disappear. But we want to know how they ended up working here, where they came from. You two might as well go back to the ship with the chopper. No point in your sticking around here. We'll be a good while, I imagine."

"But wait," Mary said. "What about Mike's boat?"

"I was coming to that," Aaron said. "We have people who will take it back to Nassau — the couple who moved into that villa you were in, the ones who were pretending to be you. It will continue the false trail, in case anybody's been keeping tabs on *Isabella*. That way, maybe nobody will connect her trip down here with your mission. Where did you leave the dinghy?"

"I beached it on Whelk Cay," Mary said.

"Okay. They can pick it up there. You two can crash on the ship for a while. Bob's planning a run to Puerto Rico. Can you find your way to *Island Girl* from there?"

"Sure," I said. "Why?"

"Mike and Bob figure you've earned a little time off, since we've interrupted your last few cruises. Where is she, anyway?"

"*Island Girl*?" Mary asked.

Aaron nodded.

"Tortola," I said. "Do I hear the chopper?"

"Yeah. Go on out to meet it. The crew knows they're taking you back to the *Lizzie Lawson*. I need to get to work scouting this place."

"Wait," Mary said. "The *Lizzie Lawson*?"

"Technically, she's the *Research Vessel Lizzie Lawson*," Aaron said.

"That's my mother's name!" Mary said.

Aaron nodded. "Yes. Bob's sister. *Lizzie's* his boat. See you two back aboard."

I stood up and took Mary's hand. "Come on, Vixen. Let's go for a helicopter ride."

EPILOGUE

Four days later in the British Virgin Islands ...

"You ready to clear out?" I asked.

Mary and I were sitting in *Island Girl's* cockpit, watching the seagulls scavenging in the anchorage at Soper's Hole. After spending the last two days provisioning and getting the boat ready for sea, we were ready to leave. Our plan was to take advantage of the northeast trade winds to sail to the Grenadines. After the four-day voyage, we would be tourists, checking out the lesser-known islands down there.

"Should we touch base with Aaron first?" Mary asked. "I'm dying of curiosity."

"Sure, why not?"

I refilled our mugs with the last of the coffee while she retrieved the Phorcys-provided satellite phone. She put the phone on the cockpit table between us and made the call.

"Finn?" Aaron's voice came from the speaker.

"And Mary," she said. "Good morning."

"Morning," Aaron said. "What's new with you two?"

"We're getting ready to leave the BVI for a while," I said. "Wondering how things were going aboard *Lizzie Lawson*."

"Any chance of a quick update?" Mary asked.

"Sure," Aaron said. "The big news is that Sergei's dead."

"Already?" I asked. "I figured you would keep him around for a while."

"Yeah. I did, too. He recovered consciousness by the time we got him back to the ship. My instructions to the team were to process him first. They cut the cuffs off, searched him, and put him in a cell. He sacked out right away — had a concussion, according to Jill. She examined him first thing, since he was wounded. Patched him up before they locked him away."

"Jill?" Mary asked. "But she's a psychiatrist."

"Yeah, but she's also a board-certified internist. A 'Jill of all trades,' so to speak. She's handy to have around."

"I guess so," Mary said. "So what happened to him?"

"The person on watch looked in on him after about an hour and found him dead. Jill's analysis is that he took a suicide pill — probably Saxitoxin — shellfish toxin."

"You said he was searched," Mary said.

"Yeah, but a lethal dose of that stuff is tiny, like the size of one-eighth of a medium sized grain of sand. And that's for an oral dose. For an injection, you're talking about a tenth of that much. So he could have had it concealed in his clothing, or in a fake mole on his skin — damn near anywhere."

"That's disappointing," I said. "There goes our information on Lavrov."

"Yeah, most likely. We're still chasing options on Sergei — fingerprints, DNA, but it won't be quick. And at best, all we'll end up with is a little more background on him. Still, it's better than nothing, and losing him will be a blow to Lavrov. We're already setting trip wires to let us spot Sergei's replacement. Plus, his loss may force Lavrov to show himself, or make some other mistake, until he can field a replacement. We'll see."

"What about the computer guy?" Mary asked.

"Greg Lewis. We can't shut him up. And he's a goldmine of information about the data centers. I'll get to that in a second, but the disappointment is that he has no clue who he was working for. He was recruited in typical computer-geek fashion — online, dark web, never met the person. Somebody called Gulliver.

"They were paying the guy a fortune, but he was oblivious to the money. They attached him to Sergei for field support, but Lewis was getting his orders from this Gulliver. He doesn't even know if Gulliver's a person or a group of people. The guy was completely wrapped up in the intellectual challenge of what he was doing. He's unconcerned about the consequences. To him, it was no different from playing a complicated online game."

"So what about the data centers?" I asked. "What were they doing with them?"

"That's the good part. Or I should say, the bad part. The short version is they were setting up for large-scale manipulation of our election results."

"Through social media, you mean?" Mary asked.

"Well, yes, but that's the least exciting part. They actually used our last election as a pilot program, and their tampering went way beyond the social media games everybody's been wringing their hands about. They altered the counts, changed the tallies of votes, but only in a few places."

"Which places?" I asked. "In the right places, that could have thrown the election, couldn't it? It was close, as it was."

"Yeah, it could have. We don't know. Lewis doesn't know

which places they hit last time around. But that was the main reason they set up the data centers. They were getting ready for the next election, and they were going for maximum impact this time."

"But wait," Mary said. "How can that be? I've read in the news that even the computerized voting machines aren't vulnerable to hacking, because they aren't online."

"Yeah, that's what they want everybody to believe. And it's true that the systems aren't vulnerable to hacking as long as they aren't online. The problem is that a lot of them *are* online, and the election officials don't always know it. That's only begun to come out in the press, and there are a lot of people working to suppress the information, for various reasons. Obviously, Lewis's employers don't want that information out, but there are people in our government trying to cover their asses, too. Some are corrupt, some are careless, and some are plain old dumb, I guess."

"I don't understand," I said. "You're saying the systems *are* online?"

"Yes, some of them are. Some of them have been, for a long time. They weren't supposed to be, but it happened. The way it's supposed to work is that each machine collects votes in its memory. A person is supposed to remove the memory card and take it to wherever the back-end system is located — for a precinct or several precincts, or a district, whatever. That varies, depending on the state. Anyway, they're supposed to hand-carry the memory card to the back-end system, where the data is read and consolidated."

"So how did the machines get online?"

"Technology offers serious temptations, and there are techies around who aren't thinking of the risks, according to Lewis. A lot of the machines have built-in wireless modems for admin control — supposed to be for basic stuff, like turning them on and off. But the techies figured out they could use the modems to collect the vote tallies. Then they figured out they could put the back-end systems online behind a secure server and automate the whole data collection process.

"There are all kinds of arguments pro and con — but mostly, it's way more efficient than having people carrying the memory cards around. Some techies argue that it's more secure. And they say they only have the systems online long enough for the transfer of data, and the data's encrypted, so it's safe. You following me?"

"Yes," Mary and I both said.

"So where's the problem?" I asked.

"The problem is that some back-end systems get left online. Either by accident, or by design, if somebody's corrupt. Once somebody hacks into one, they have a toehold. The hackers can modify the code that controls the back-end system. Then once they're inside, they can spread the modifications across other parts of the system.

"Those data centers Lewis was managing were doing all kinds of support work. But Gulliver's big plan was that by the next election, their server farms would fool the back-end systems. Instead of collecting data from voting machines, the back-end systems would be fed vote counts from the Russian-controlled servers."

"Whoa," I said. "And they wouldn't need to alter the counts everywhere — only in certain critical places, right?"

"Right. And Gulliver is running analysis programs all the time. He tells Lewis which election precincts are the most critical."

"Did Lewis help your team get access to the data center in Miami?" Mary asked.

"Yes. That one's under our control, now."

"So you've put the brakes on Gulliver," I said.

"Maybe, but Lewis thinks Gulliver may have other people like him, running other server farms."

"What's your next step, then?"

"We're still putting the pieces together. There are several options, including fielding hackers of our own. We have a little time before the next national election. We're pretty sure we can shut down the tampering. The problem will be the aftershocks when all the corrupt players realize the game's up. All hell will break loose. Stay tuned; I have a feeling there will be more work for you two."

"It almost seems anticlimactic," Mary said. "But what about the other prisoners?"

"Well, all of them except Grissom outlived their usefulness. They were just vermin; they've been dealt with."

"Except Grissom?" I asked.

"Yeah. Turns out Grissom is an undercover FBI agent."

"Damn!" I said.

"And what was he doing?" Mary asked.

"He was supposed to be infiltrating what was left of O'Hanlon's operation, trying to get a handle on who was taking it over. At least that's his story."

"You sound doubtful," I said.

"Well, yeah."

"Can't you find out if he's really an FBI agent?" Mary asked.

"Oh, he's really an FBI agent," Aaron said. "That still leaves two questions. The first one is whether he's crooked."

"And the second one?" Mary asked.

"Is whether his chain of command can be trusted. We're working on it, but it will take a little time. Meanwhile, Grissom's cooling his heels on *Lizzie*."

After a few seconds of silence, I asked, "Anything else for us?"

"Not right now. Keep that satellite phone close, though. It will probably be a couple of weeks before we've sorted through everything. Mike and Bob were serious about you guys taking a break, so I won't bug you until they ask me to. But one of them might want to talk with you. Have a good time sailing, and stay safe."

"Thanks, Aaron," I said.

"Yes, thanks," Mary said. "You take care."

And with that, we disconnected the call.

"You know what?" Mary asked.

"What?"

"I'm glad we're getting some time to go sailing like regular people, you old villain."

"I am, too, Vixen. Let's go chase a few sunsets."

The End

MAILING LIST

THANK YOU FOR READING *VILLAINS AND VIXENS*.

SIGN up for my mailing list at http://eepurl.com/bKujyv for notice of new releases and special sales or giveaways. I'll email a link to you for a free download of my short story, The Lost Tourist Franchise, when you sign up. I promise not to use the list for anything else; I dislike spam as much as you do.

A NOTE TO THE READER

Thank you again for reading *Villains and Vixens,* the fifth book in the **J.R. Finn Sailing Mystery Series.** The next book in the series will be released later in 2021. Please sign up for my mailing list for more information on release dates.

Reviews are of great benefit to independent authors like me; they help me more than you can imagine. They are a primary means to help new readers find my work. A few words from you can help others find the pleasure that I hope you found in this book, as well as keeping my spirits up as I work on the next one.

The **J.R. Finn Sailing Mystery Series** is available in paperback and in audiobook format. Learn more about these audiobooks on my website.

I also write two other sailing-thriller series set in the Caribbean. If you enjoyed the adventures of Finn and Mary, you'll enjoy the **Bluewater Thrillers** and the **Connie Barrera Thrillers**.

The **Bluewater Thrillers** feature two young women, Dani Berger and Liz Chirac. Dani and Liz sail a luxury charter yacht named *Vengeance*. They often find trouble, but they can take care of themselves.

The **Connie Barrera Thrillers** are a spin-off from the **Bluewater Thrillers**. Before Connie went to sea, she was a first-rate con artist. Dani and Liz met Connie in *Bluewater Ice*, and they taught her to sail. She liked it so much she bought a charter yacht of her own.

Dani and Liz also introduced her to Paul Russo, a retired Miami homicide detective. Paul signed on as her first mate and chef, but he ended up as her husband. Connie and Paul run a charter sailing yacht named *Diamantista*. Like Dani and Liz, they're often beset by problems unrelated to sailing.

The **Bluewater Thrillers** and the **Connie Barrera Thrillers** share many of the same characters. Phillip Davis and his wife Sandrine, Sharktooth, and Marie LaCroix often appear in both series, as do Connie, Paul, Dani, and Liz. Here's a link to the web page that lists those novels in order of publication: http://www.clrdougherty.com/p/bluewater-thrillers-and-connie-barrera.html

---

A list of all my books is on the last page; just click on a title or go to my website for more information. If you'd like to know when my next book is released, visit my author's page on Amazon at www.amazon.com/author/clrdougherty and click the "Follow" link or sign up for my mailing list at http://eepurl.com/bKujyv for information on sales and special promotions.

I welcome email correspondence about books, boats and sailing. My address is clrd@clrdougherty.com. I enjoy hearing from people who read my books; I always answer email from readers. Thanks again for your support.

ABOUT THE AUTHOR

Welcome Aboard!

Charles Dougherty is a lifelong sailor; he's lived what he writes. He and his wife have spent over 30 years sailing together.

For 15 years, they lived aboard their boat full-time, cruising the East Coast and the Caribbean islands. They spent most of that time exploring the Eastern Caribbean.

Dougherty is well acquainted with the islands and their people. The characters and locations in his novels reflect his experience.

A storyteller before all else, Dougherty lets his characters speak for themselves. Pick up one of his thrillers and listen to the sound of adventure as you smell the salt air. Enjoy the views of distant horizons and meet some people you won't forget.

Dougherty's sailing fiction books include the **Bluewater Thrillers**, the **Connie Barrera Thrillers**, and the **J.R. Finn Sailing Mysteries**.

Dougherty's first novel was *Deception in Savannah*. While it's not about sailing, one of the main characters is Connie Barrera. He had so much fun with Connie that he built a sailing series around her.

Before writing Connie's series, he wrote the first three

Bluewater Thrillers, about two young women running a charter yacht in the islands. In the fourth book, Connie shows up as their charter guest.

She stayed for the fifth Bluewater book. Then Connie demanded her own series.

The J.R. Finn books are his newest sailing series. The first Finn book, though it begins in Puerto Rico, starts with a real-life encounter that Dougherty had in St. Lucia. For more information about that, visit his website.

Dougherty's other fiction works are the *Redemption of Becky Jones*, a psycho-thriller, and *The Lost Tourist Franchise*, a short story about another of the characters from *Deception in Savannah*.

Dougherty has also written two non-fiction books. *Life's a Ditch* is the story of how he and his wife moved aboard their sailboat, Play Actor, and their adventures along the east coast of the U.S. *Dungda de Islan'* relates their experiences while cruising the Caribbean.

Charles Dougherty welcomes email correspondence with readers.

www.clrdougherty.com
clrd@clrdougherty.com

OTHER BOOKS BY C.L.R. DOUGHERTY

Bluewater Thrillers

Bluewater Killer

Bluewater Vengeance

Bluewater Voodoo

Bluewater Ice

Bluewater Betrayal

Bluewater Stalker

Bluewater Bullion

Bluewater Rendezvous

Bluewater Ganja

Bluewater Jailbird

Bluewater Drone

Bluewater Revolution

Bluewater Enigma

Bluewater Quest

Bluewater Target

Bluewater Blackmail

Bluewater Clickbait

Bluewater Thrillers Boxed Set: Books 1-3

Connie Barrera Thrillers

From Deception to Betrayal - An Introduction to Connie Barrera

Love for Sail - A Connie Barrera Thriller

Sailor's Delight - A Connie Barrera Thriller

A Blast to Sail - A Connie Barrera Thriller

Storm Sail - A Connie Barrera Thriller

Running Under Sail - A Connie Barrera Thriller

Sails Job - A Connie Barrera Thriller

Under Full Sail - A Connie Barrera Thriller

An Easy Sail - A Connie Barrera Thriller

A Torn Sail - A Connie Barrera Thriller

A Righteous Sail - A Connie Barrera Thriller

Sailor Take Warning - A Connie Barrera Thriller

Sailor's Choice - A Connie Barrera Thriller

J.R. Finn Sailing Mysteries

Assassins and Liars

Avengers and Rogues

Vigilantes and Lovers

Sailors and Sirens

Villains and Vixens

Killers and Keepers

Devils and Divas

Sharks and Prey

Other Fiction

Deception in Savannah

The Redemption of Becky Jones

The Lost Tourist Franchise

Books for Sailors and Dreamers

Life's a Ditch

Dungda de Islan'

Audiobooks

Assassins and Liars

Avengers and Rogues

Vigilantes and Lovers

Sailors and Sirens

Villains and Vixens

Killers and Keepers

Devils and Divas

Sharks and Prey

For more information please visit www.clrdougherty.com

Or visit www.amazon.com/author/clrdougherty

Made in the USA
Monee, IL
20 August 2021